Blizzard Besties

YAMILE SAIED MÉNDEZ

Scholastic Inc.

10 9 8 7 6 5 4 3 2 1   19 20 21 22 23

Printed in Dongguan, China   163
First printing 2019

Book design by Jennifer Rinaldi

To the memory of Beatriz
Aurora López, the
best Mami and
Yaya ever.

And to Jeffrey, for everything.

Chapter One
Disaster Magnet

Despite her record, Vanesa Campos was determined not to ruin her family's vacation. Not this special one. Since getting off the airplane, nothing major had happened, but a whole week stretched out ahead that could turn into disaster. She could feel a catastrophe sneaking up on her.

She was wearing a million layers, but goose bumps covered her arms. Her ears popped. Maybe they did because the minibus was going full speed down a mountain road across Parley's Canyon. They were headed toward Park City, Utah—and, hopefully, the world's greatest ski vacation. Vanesa had her eyes shut so she wouldn't get carsick. She twisted her new friendship bracelet between her fingers. It was the ugliest shade of brown in the world. Amber had promised Vanesa that after the break she could have a golden bracelet—*if* she became an official Sunshine Darling.

The shuttle came to a sudden stop, and the driver exclaimed, "Welcome to Pinecloud Lodge!"

Right on cue, Vanesa's phone vibrated in her pocket, announcing the arrival of an avalanche of messages.

She sneaked her phone out carefully and peeked at the screen. Seeing that her notifications were in the double digits, she whispered, "Finally!" She also added a silent prayer of thanks to the internet fairies. The *PinecloudGuests* Wi-Fi had three solid bars, which guaranteed uninterrupted connection to her friends. If she broke her perfect message streak with the group, her chance for permanent membership in the Darlings would vanish—she was already on probation.

She had to reply to all her messages, but that would have to wait a little longer. She slipped her phone back into her pocket.

From the seat beside her, Mami pressed Vanesa's free hand affectionately and smiled.

"Finally!" she echoed.

Vanesa pressed her mom's hand back. In the seat ahead, Papi looked over his shoulder and gave them a thumbs-up, grinning like a little kid. Vanesa knew that her parents had been saving up for a long time for this *real* vacation—one that wasn't just visiting family.

Hunter, her little brother, who sat next to Papi, turned around, his head popping over the seat. He spoke in a whisper that for sure carried to all the passengers. "Remember," he said to Vanesa, "let's not ruin this vacation. And when I say *let's*, I mean *don't*. I've never been on a real vacation before, and I'm seven-and-three-quarters years old already!"

Papi, Mami, and Vanesa cringed, but Hunter was too cute to tell off. Besides, he was only voicing everyone's biggest concern. Luckily, Papi urged him to turn around again, shooting Vanesa an apologetic smile that didn't make her feel any better.

Vanesa *did* have a reputation for ruining family outings. Unintentionally, of course, but still . . .

Last year, Vanesa had gotten sick with the stomach flu on the way to Christmas Eve dinner at Tío Pablo's in Pasadena. Papi had to turn the car around half an hour before they reached their destination. By the time they arrived back home in Las Flores, all four members of the Campos family were hurling. It hadn't technically been Vanesa's fault, but she'd been the one to start the Great Winter Plague that lasted for weeks. Also, if she'd listened to her gut carefully (and literally), she could've told Mami that the growling didn't mean good news. But she'd kept quiet.

The year before that, when she was only ten, Vanesa tripped on her cousin's enormous dress in her eagerness to pull a ribbon from the quinceañera cake. Seconds before the cake-pocalypse, a little voice in the back of Vanesa's mind had told her to wait patiently, but she wanted to get the ring hidden in the cake. She hadn't listened and ended up covered in meringue and dulce de leche. Her cousin *eventually* forgave her, but it would be a while before Vanesa, her parents, and Hunter were invited back to join the family in Miami for any kind of party.

The worst memory of all, though, was of that unforgettable, unforgivable, unmentionable day on her twelfth birthday last fall when her mistake had almost cost her a friend *and* hurt her little brother. She always shivered when she thought of that afternoon.

The day after that disaster, Abuela Bea had sat down next to Vanesa and told her that next time she had a feeling, she should listen to it. Sometimes the feeling was one's wiser inner self, or an angel, sending a warning.

But Vanesa didn't believe in immaterial things like warnings from angels. She could never really trust herself again after so many mistakes! Right then and there, she promised she wouldn't—she couldn't—let her little brother, Hunter, out of her sight that way again.

Hunter needed all the help he could get to stay out of trouble.

Vanesa watched Hunter spring to his feet when the shuttle driver, who looked like Santa Claus with a coonskin hat, gave the passengers the go-ahead to disembark. Hunter rushed down the bus steps ahead of everyone else.

"Hunter, put your jacket on!" Mami exclaimed. "You're going to get a cold!" She ran after Hunter, shaking his bright yellow jacket in her hand. With his asthma, even a little cough was bad news. Here in Park City, the sun shone brightly, but Vanesa remembered her phone had said the temperatures were barely in the two-digit range. When it came to Hunter's health, they couldn't take any chances.

From her seat next to the window, Vanesa saw her little brother make a beeline for the main entrance to the lodge, his curly brown hair like a bird's nest after the flight from California and the drive from the airport. Mami smashed the nestlike hair with a multicolored hat. Hunter pulled it off, and Mami gently ushered him toward the wood-and-glass doors of Pinecloud Lodge. A green flag with the logo—the outline of a cabin with a big dog guarding it—flapped in the wind.

Vanesa was pleasantly surprised at how fancy Pinecloud Lodge looked. She'd have plenty of photo ops to wow Amber and the Darlings. The main building was an enormous, brand-new log cabin. Tucked behind it, the much-smaller original cabin, built back in the 1800s or something, was now the headquarters for the kids' club—or so the website advertised. Out of all the fun winter activities at the lodge, Vanesa couldn't wait to impress her family with her skiing skills. She'd only skied once before (when she was seven), but she'd been so good, she was sure this time she'd be exceptional. And after skiing all day, she'd drink hot chocolate topped with butterscotch marshmallows. At night, she'd watch the blinking stars from the fluffiest bed in the world.

Judging by his excitement, Hunter couldn't wait, either. As he got closer to the doors, he nearly ran into a fashionable blond girl not much older than Vanesa. The girl kept walking, a gigantic glittery makeup case in one hand and a book in the other. Her long bright-pink coat fluttered behind her like a cape. Vanesa thought she recognized her from somewhere. Maybe an online tutorial? A YouTube show? She couldn't tell from so far away. The girl had a glamorous glow. A lot of famous people came to Park City for vacation. Maybe Vanesa would make friends with a celebrity.

A teenage boy with a green plaid vest like the bus driver's was sprinkling salt on the icy sidewalk. He hurried to help the incoming passengers down the bus steps and slipped on the ice himself, barely keeping his balance by swinging his arms like a windmill. The glamorous girl didn't even seem to notice. Vanesa chuckled.

The bus was mostly empty by now, and Papi called to her from near the front of the bus. "Let's go, Vane." He pronounced her nickname the Spanish way: *VAH-neh*. "Ready to have a blast?"

Vanesa smiled at him briefly, but she'd just received a request via text from the Darlings.

Be a Darling, send a picture of the lodge.

This was message number thirteen, and she *had* to respond. Amber, Rory, and Peyton were at Amber's aunt's house in Florida for break. Pinecloud wasn't sunny Miami, but it was still pretty to Vanesa. She snapped a picture of the white-covered mountains and buildings against the turquoise sky. She captioned it *Winter wonderland* and sent it.

Her heart pounded as she waited for a reply.

"Do you guys come to Utah to ski often?" the driver asked. When he turned sideways to make room for passengers to slip by him on their way off the bus, Vanesa read his name tag: ZACHARIAH.

Papi laughed. "We're not exactly winter people, but Vanesa here loves to ski."

"Is that right?" Zachariah asked. "With your tan, I took you for a regular California girl."

Vanesa would've replied that her skin wasn't tanned— her skin was naturally brown—or that a California girl was totally allowed to love both the beach and the snow. But she was distracted by her phone's buzz in her pocket. She looked down at her friends' replies: three different versions of the Sleepwalker meme—a girl flailing as she fell into a pool.

Nightmare. We hate winter, said Amber's caption.

Rory and Peyton only did whatever Amber said, so Amber's reply stung the most.

"Vane, put the phone away. What did Mami say?" Papi urged her forward with a nod of his head.

Mami had been clear, and Papi had agreed: At the first sign of disobedience, excessive rowdiness, or obsessive checking of her messages, the phone would be gone like *that.* The snap of Mami's fingers still resonated in Vanesa's ears. She couldn't take any risks. She put her phone back into her pocket and stepped off the bus.

The cold air was a shock. Vanesa loved the smell of winter—clearest blue. She inhaled deeply and smiled with satisfaction at the crunching sound the snow made under her sneakers. Her phone vibrated in her pocket again. She looked down to check it as she walked into the lobby.

She never got to read the message because she crashed into someone blocking the entrance.

"Hey, watch it!" It was the glamorous blond girl Vanesa had seen earlier.

"I'm so sorry," Vanesa said. She clutched her phone so she wouldn't drop it and crack the screen.

The girl gasped as her eyes swept over Vanesa. She looked disgusted, horrified. Did Vanesa have antlers or something?

"This is a total disaster!" she said in a strangled voice.

Vanesa wasn't sure what she'd done to offend the girl so much. When she put her phone back in her pocket, she touched a piece of candy she'd saved from the flight. She pulled it out and offered it to the girl. "Sorry, do you want a piece of candy?"

The girl scoffed and stepped back.

To be sure, Vanesa brushed her hand over her head. No. No antlers there. Before she could ask what was wrong, Hunter ran over to them. Without missing a beat, he exclaimed, "You guys are wearing exactly the same clothes!" and started laughing while pointing at them.

Chapter Two
Enemies—Oh, Deer!

As soon as the words were out of Hunter's mouth, Vanesa realized that under her black jacket she was wearing the exact same thing as the girl in front of her. Since she'd thought the girl was fashionable, a surge of warmth bloomed inside her. Vanesa had nailed her travel outfit: dark jeans, gray sweater, and black sneakers. But the blond girl had a pop of color with her pink coat. Vanesa owned a pink jacket, too, but if Amber or the rest of the Darlings saw her wearing such a babyish color, she would be in trouble.

The girl walked away with an irritated huff before Vanesa could say something to smooth out the situation. She was a total diva, and Vanesa loved her instantly.

Mami, who was standing by the check-in counter, called Vanesa to her side. "I saw you bump into that girl because you weren't looking. Don't let me see you with that phone or else."

Vanesa didn't dare argue back.

Mami turned to wag a finger at Hunter. "And you, mister. Stop running like a chicken with its head cut off or you'll be in trouble, too. Vas a ver."

Hunter sent Vanesa a look of sympathy that she returned. From experience, she knew what there was *to see* after Mami's threat—nothing good. Usually extra homework, or worse, chores.

Vanesa held Hunter's tiny, sweaty hand as Papi and Mami checked in. Immediately, Hunter let go of her hand to point at someone. "Is he the driver's twin?" he whisper-shouted.

Everyone in the lobby turned to follow his pointed index finger.

Next to one of the fireplaces stood another Santa Claus-y man. JOSIAH, according to his tag. He wore a red foxtail hat on top of bushy white hair. Vanesa hoped the fur was fake, but she wouldn't bet on it.

"Maybe they're brothers," Papi said. He gestured to a line of portraits that hung on the lobby wall. Every person in the pictures had the same unruly hair as Zachariah's and Josiah's, even the scary-looking woman on a black horse whose portrait hung in the center of the wall. "Looks like everyone in these portraits is family, too."

The concierge, a pale, thin man with shiny black hair and a neat mustache, nodded and said, "Josiah and Zachariah Grant? You're correct, sir: They are brothers. This is a family-run establishment."

"Oh, you're their brother, too? But you look nothing like them!" Hunter said, scratching his head.

Vanesa's dad smiled and said, "Not a bit of shyness in this one."

"It's okay, amiguinho," the man with the mustache said. "I'm Luís Sanches, the daytime concierge. I'm not a Grant, but I'm still here to serve."

"You speak Spanish?" Hunter asked with wonder in his voice.

Luís snapped his fingers. "Portuguese. A close cousin." The phone rang, and he added, "Excuse me, I need to take this. Pinecloud," he said into the phone receiver, "how may I help you?"

"He speaks Porgutese," Hunter said in another of those whispers that everyone could hear. He looked at Papi with eyes like a Beanie Boo's, throwing warmth all around. Everyone in the lobby tried to hide their amusement behind their hands. There was no contest. Hunter was the cutest kid ever. Even the diva in the pink coat smiled back at him; although when she noticed Vanesa watching, the humor in her eyes vanished.

"Welcome, welcome," Josiah Grant's voice boomed. He seemed oblivious to the warning look Luís sent him as he shielded the phone receiver with his hand. "We're pleased to welcome our first guests since our big renovation. Look, you're so special even Rocky's here to meet you in person."

Vanesa followed the direction of Josiah's pointing finger. Next to a fireplace sat . . . a bear? She took several steps back and yelped. Everyone in the group laughed when she tripped against Papi's suitcase. Vanesa was too terrified to worry about her bruised ego.

Her heart was still pounding hard in her ears when she realized that what she'd thought was a bear was in fact a dog. A gigantic dog. A mountain of dog. The black-and-white, fur-covered beast practically reached Josiah's elbow!

"Cool!" exclaimed a Black girl of around twelve. She ran to the dog, and a Black boy who looked like he must be her brother said, "Wait for me, Emma!"

Vanesa studied the siblings. Their deep brown skin was a little darker than Vanesa's. The girl was taller than the boy. She wore beads at the ends of her long braided hair, which was brown mixed with a shade of purple that clashed with the puffy orange jacket she wore. The boy's hair was buzzed short. The two of them argued about who'd reached the dog first and had dibs on petting. While they were distracted, Hunter cut in front of them and hugged the dog as if they were soul mates already.

"Gentle, Hunter. Cuidado," Mami warned. Sometimes Hunter's allergies flared up when he petted an animal.

The dog was already happily licking Hunter's face, while Hunter said, "That's a good boy. What a good boy you are!"

All that hair.

All that dog spit.

Vanesa almost gagged.

She knew not all dogs were the same, and this one had hopefully been trained to protect people, not chase them.

Still, her mind flashed to the big German shepherd that had chased her in the park when she was younger than Hunter was now. She only liked tiny dogs, and she shuddered at the thought of those heavy paws, those sharp teeth.

Vanesa skirted around the dog to avoid catching his attention and stood next to one of the oversize fireplaces. She had the urge to check her messages, but Mami's eye was on her, so she pulled her hand away from her pocket as if she'd gotten an electric shock.

"I'm sorry for the delay in checking you in," Luís said to the grown-ups. "The calls keep dropping. Looks like this approaching storm might be bigger than anyone expected."

Some of the adults, including Mami and Papi, exchanged alarmed looks.

Josiah noticed everyone's concern and announced, "We're absolutely safe in Pinecloud. This storm is great news for those who love winter."

Vanesa and Hunter's high five echoed loudly.

Josiah laughed. "High fives all around!" He went across the room high-fiving the kids. "We haven't gotten much snow yet this winter. We need all we can get."

Luís hung up the phone and turned to the Camposes. "Let me help you, Senhor Campos," he said.

While Luís checked her family in, Vanesa looked around the lobby, bubbling with excitement. A storm meant fresh snow. Pinecloud was the perfect place to be in the wintertime. Not that she'd say that to Amber, who hadn't appreciated the picture Vanesa had sent. But then, not even the professional pictures on the website did the resort justice. The inside of the cabin was magnificent. Under a few evergreen garlands, the dark wood of the desk and staircases gleamed like they had been recently polished. Some of the garlands were decorated with photos in tiny frames, which seemed to be of past lodge guests.

Although a storm was in the forecast, the sun still shone brightly through the thick-paned windows, and dust motes swirled in a sunbeam. Portraits hung above the fireplaces; many of them featured that fierce-looking woman Vanesa had already noticed—in some she was younger, riding horses, a llama, and even an ostrich. In others, she was older, but still had that youthful smirk on her face. Some were paintings and some were black-and-white photos, but in each, her eyes glowed like a fire. Vanesa wanted to know more about her.

Hunter had gone back to playing with the dog, but the other kids, including the diva, milled around a wooden sled filled with stuffed animals: ostriches, deer, bunnies, llamas, moose, wolves, and tiny replicas of the dog who had already become Hunter's best friend.

The big black dog was sprawled on the floor, tongue lolling to the side. Hunter tried to climb him like a horse but finally slid off the dog's back and tickled his white tummy. The dog's leg shook, which made him look like he was playing a guitar. The boy with the short hair noticed how much fun those two were having, and after snatching a stuffed beaver, he joined Hunter in tickling the dog's sides. Dogs didn't laugh of course, but this one had the most content expression on his face.

Josiah Grant motioned toward the sled with the stuffed animals and said, "Go ahead, girls. You're welcome to choose a friend for your stay."

Vanesa, the girl named Emma, and the diva all reached down at the same time to get a stuffed animal. Vanesa grabbed two: one for her and one for Hunter. In one hand, she had a dog. In the other, the one holding the last available baby deer, she felt a tug of resistance.

The diva's eyes lasered in on Vanesa, and Vanesa dropped the deer.

"Sorry," she said, although there was nothing to be sorry for. Was it her fault that they liked the exact same one? In Vanesa's mind, it only meant they had lots in common. They both wore awesome clothes and were lovers of adorable baby deer. Why was this girl looking at her with so much disgust?

The diva sneered. "Nah, you can have it. I don't want it anymore." She tossed the deer back into the sled and, without even looking at the animals, picked up another one, a dog.

Vanesa didn't know what to say. Should she keep the deer or insist that the other girl take it?

The girl stood with a hand on her hip and her chin lifted in the air, like she was challenging Vanesa to a duel or something.

An older-looking lady by the concierge's desk was trying

to get the diva's attention. She held the glittery makeup case in her hand. "Beck!" she called, and waved.

Trying to be helpful, Vanesa said, "I think your grandma is calling you."

The girl—Beck—looked over her shoulder at the lady calling her. Then she whipped around to glare at Vanesa with such hatred that Vanesa stepped back in fear.

"She's my mom, you . . . you . . . airhead!" Beck spit out the words.

"I'm sorry," Vanesa said. "I'm sorry."

Beck had already stomped away to her mom.

Vanesa wished the earth would open up and swallow her. Her phone danced in her pocket, but she was too upset to look at the messages.

"Don't mind her," the girl with the purple braids said, interrupting Vanesa's thoughts. "I'm Emma. What's your name?" She smiled so warmly, Vanesa couldn't help but smile back.

"I'm Vanesa," she said, and pushed down the knot in her throat.

Emma grabbed the deer and handed it to Vanesa. "It seems our brothers are already best friends."

The two boys were having fun making the dog roll on command.

Vanesa shrugged one shoulder, still hurt by Beck's reaction. "I guess little brothers can be fun . . . sometimes."

"Actually," Emma said, cringing, "Eric and I are twins."

Vanesa's face went hot. Why did she keep saying the wrong thing? If she offended Emma, she wouldn't have any friends during her stay at the lodge.

Luckily, Emma didn't seem to mind. She playfully slapped Vanesa in the arm and said, "He's only three whole minutes older, though. He never lets me forget it." She inched closer to Vanesa and whispered, "Don't let him hear you say he looks younger. He's super self-conscious that I'm already taller than him." Unlike Hunter, Emma knew how to whisper without letting the whole room hear.

Vanesa mimed sealing her lips and throwing away the key. Emma laughed loudly. Her voice sounded like a bell.

"Yikes! I don't want your brother to hate me. I can't make another enemy," Vanesa said, looking in the direction where Beck and her mom had gone. "That girl Beck hates me!"

Emma draped an arm over her shoulder and said, "Don't worry about her. Hey, are you coming to ski class later?"

Vanesa's mood brightened just thinking about being out in the snow for their first ski class. "Of course! After I unpack and . . . get things organized, I'll meet you there." She didn't add that she needed to reply to the group chat messages. Once again, she was grateful for strong Wi-Fi.

"Deal! See you in a couple of hours," Emma said, and she followed her parents, who were calling to her and Eric from the top of the stairs.

"Perfect," Vanesa said to herself. Two hours would give her enough time to catch up on the Darlings' messages. She had to reply to every message within the same day, and she was so behind already! Hopefully Amber wouldn't be mad at her.

"Vane! Hunter!" Papi called. He waved, holding up a map and a small envelope that looked like it contained a key card.

The last time they'd stayed at a hotel, her parents had rented a family suite. Vanesa got the queen bed in the smaller room, and Hunter slept in the trundle in the small living room that connected the two bedrooms. He hadn't complained because he got to sleep in front of the TV; he'd also been younger and hadn't cared. But now that he was older, the usual arrangements might be in danger.

She ran to grab her key card before Hunter got ahold of it. She had an advantage because he first had to detangle himself from the fluffy dog's embrace.

Papi handed Vanesa the envelope and said, "One key for you and one for Hunter. They're for room 207. Ours is 208."

"Two rooms?"

Her dad tsked and gave a small shrug. "They only have one suite, and it's unavailable. So Mamá and I decided to get two adjacent rooms. One for you guys and one for us."

Vanesa wanted to do a happy dance. She'd be able to stay on the group chat even after bedtime. She'd just have to let Hunter play *DragonVille* on her phone at some point so he wouldn't go to Mami with the gossip.

Before she noticed what was happening, Hunter weaved between Vanesa and Papi and grabbed the key cards from Vanesa's hand. "Sweet! I get to sleep in a fluffy bed, too!" he exclaimed, jumping up and down. Dog hair covered his jeans and sweater. Gross!

Vanesa tried to snatch the keys back, but Hunter dodged her and ran ahead, laughing.

"Give it back, Hunter!" She darted after him, but Mami stopped her in her tracks with one freezing look.

"Remember. One strike and the phone is gone. Please, don't stress me out before my massage."

Heavyhearted, Vanesa made an effort to match Mami's stride instead of chasing her brother like she wanted to. Why did Mami have to walk so slowly? Didn't she have a massage to get to?

They finally reached their hallway. "I'll see you later," Mami said, kissing her on the cheek. Vanesa didn't return the kiss, and Mami added, "Vane, have a good attitude, baby. Let's start on the right foot."

Vanesa waited for her mom to get through the door before mumbling, "Easy for you to say!" She sighed. Mami was right. Maybe there would be two beds—then none of this would matter.

But when she walked into the room she had to share with Hunter, she gasped in horror. On the one and only gloriously enormous king-size bed lay Hunter—in his dog hair–covered clothes.

He gave her an infuriatingly smug grin and said, "Taken!"

Chapter Three
BRB

Vanesa tried negotiating with Hunter for the bed without success.

"I got it first," he said, and did that thing where he made his body extra heavy so Vanesa couldn't move him—not even when she pulled on his leg with all her might. She sat on the floor and tried all her tricks, from threatening to promising to pretend-crying. Hunter wouldn't budge.

"You won't win, Vanesa. I want to be comfy, too."

"Number one," Vanesa said, "I'm the oldest and I had dibs. Number two, I got you a stuffed dog."

She threw the stuffed animal at Hunter. He caught it with one hand and hugged it against his chest. "Aw, aren't you fluffy?" Then he looked back stone-faced at Vanesa and said, "It won't work."

Vanesa huffed and puffed and continued listing the reasons she deserved the bed. When she was on number seventeen (being the first person in their family to make the honor roll *and* the middle-school basketball team, which Amber wanted her to switch for cheer, but Vanesa wasn't going to mention *that*), someone knocked on the door. The words hardened in her mouth. She heard her heart beating like a drum in her ears.

You. Are. Doomed.

You. Are. Doomed.

"That's them," Hunter said with that aggravating smirk while he wiggled his skinny body and messed up the perfectly laid covers. "Remember, Mami said not to make them stressed before their 'hot-stone massage.'" He made quote signs with his fingers.

"Hunter!" Vanesa glared at her little brother. "Give me the bed, and I'll forget all about you being horrible!"

Hunter opened his mouth to reply when there was another knock.

"Chicos," Papi said. "We can't be late to our massage. Open up."

Vanesa stomped to the door and opened it dramatically, hoping her parents would put Hunter in his place: the sofa bed.

"Mami, Hunter—"

Vanesa stopped talking as soon as she saw her parents. Mami and Papi were wearing the lodge's comfy cream-colored robes. Mami was smiling widely, as if the promise of a massage in the near future was already working its magic. Vanesa didn't want to be the one ruining this for her. Mami deserved some peace and quiet, and Hunter didn't get it.

But her parents must have had supernatural senses or something. Maybe Vanesa's face wasn't as cheerful as she thought it was. As soon as her mom took a look at the situation, she raised her hands, and said, "Now don't start fighting, guys. We came all the way here to relax and decompress. No family drama, please!"

"But, Mami! It's not fair," Vanesa said, her determination to be good forgotten. "I should sleep on the big bed. I'm the girl." She looked at her dad for moral support. Usually, he took her side in this kind of argument.

"What about gender equality?" Hunter counterattacked. "You're always going on about that."

"Sweetheart, this is such a first-world problem," Papi said, placing a hand on Vanesa's shoulder. She made an effort not to roll her eyes. "You two need to figure this out."

"But—"

"No buts," Papi said, and Hunter laughed like the immature seven-year-old he was. "Seriously," Papi continued, trying to keep a straight face. "Promise me you two won't fight."

"Or the phone is gone, remember . . . ," Mami said, leaving her warning bouncing in Vanesa's ears.

"Promise," Hunter and Vanesa reluctantly chanted.

The half-hearted effort must have been good enough for Papi because he saluted and said, "Mami and I are out. Don't forget your ski class," he added. He took Mami gently by the elbow, and they left the room.

At the same moment, Vanesa's phone buzzed, and she looked down instinctively to check the notifications. Ten more missed messages. Amber would be furious. She had to reply right now.

By the time Vanesa looked back up, her parents were long gone, and with them her chance of getting what she wanted: the bed. She stood at the door, all her words crowded in her mouth. When she turned around to face her brother, Hunter grinned at her like he'd pulled the hugest prank in the universe.

"You're horrible," she said, putting all the emphasis on *horrible*.

Hunter threw her a kiss and pointed at the TV with the remote. Somehow, like an expert, he immediately found one of his shows, the one with the ninjas of every color of the rainbow.

She'd been so nice to him the whole day, letting him play on her phone and giving him the window seat on the airplane. And he didn't care that she'd been planning on this day for the last two years. Every night since her parents had told them about Pinecloud, after homework and all her chores were done, Vanesa had gone on the website and studied the schedule for the kids' lodge activities. She'd fantasized about finally getting back on a ski slope and relaxing in the lodge.

Now Hunter had claimed her bed, and she'd promised her parents not to fight.

"Hunter, please . . ."

He yawned so wide, his jaw popped. "The bed's huge. We can share. Come watch ninjas with me." He patted the bed.

"I'm not sharing a bed with you," she mumbled as she yanked the cushions off the sofa to make her bed. The mattress was so thin, she could see the impression of the coils on the sheets. "I'm sick and tired of you, Hunter. I hate hanging out with you."

Hunter did that whimpery sound he always did when he wanted to get away with acting like a brat or make Vanesa feel like the worst sister in the world. This time she wouldn't play along.

In fact, she would play her own game. She stomped toward the TV and turned the volume all the way down. Hunter must have felt a little guilty because he didn't complain. Good. It was about time he started behaving like a big boy.

She sat on the bed and started replying to her messages and telling her friends how lucky they were not to be stuck with a small pest of a brother while their parents left her babysitting. Which wasn't exactly true, but venting made her feel better.

The sound of a growling bear made her jump. She looked around for the beast that had made such a noise and realized it was Hunter snoring.

He was out cold. How long had she been on her phone? She'd totally lost track of time. Soon they'd have to head to their ski class.

Vanesa watched Hunter's sleeping face. When he was asleep, he did seem like an angel, what with the long eyelashes that cast shadows on his cheeks and the hair curling around his ears.

She'd lost the war. Now she'd have to make do with the flat mattress and the worn sheets that had survived the renovations all over the lodge. But she'd keep her phone at least.

Vanesa wandered over to the desk and picked up the sheet that listed the schedule of Kids' Activities. The mornings and afternoons were reserved for skiing, snowshoeing, sledding, and snowman-building competitions. Marshmallows and hot cocoa by the fire pit followed dinner. Movies, arcade games, foosball and Ping-Pong competitions, and karaoke completed the days.

Vanesa felt her spirits lift. If she chose to, she could spend all day with other kids, away from her parents' watchful eyes! She'd have to bring Hunter along to everything, but she was sure he'd find kids his age to keep him company. If not, Rocky the dog would distract him.

She thought back to the last time she'd skied—that one wonderful trip that came before her unlucky curse of ruining every vacation. It had been years since she'd felt the rush of wind on her face, the crunch of snow under her skis, the speed of going down the mountain.

Pinecloud was a small lodge—it only had two buildings. But it shared skiing facilities, including a chairlift to the top of the most fun ski runs, with a few other lodges and hotels. Vanesa got butterflies in her stomach imagining herself atop the mountain above the trees, close to the bright blue sky before she skied down the slopes like the Olympians she admired.

She snapped a picture of the activities sheet and sent it to the Sunshine Darlings.

Seconds later, a new set of three thumbs-down arrived in quick succession. Right after, she got a video of Amber, Peyton, and Rory at the pool. The three girls' golden hair shone under the sun, and their smiles stretched from ear to ear. They wore matching black swimsuits with golden accents, like they were part of a synchronized swim team. Their golden bracelets glinted in the sun.

If only she had a cool friend to spend this week at the lodge with!

At least Emma, the twin, had been super nice to her, and who knew? Maybe Beck would have a change of heart and give her a second chance.

With small hopes for making friends, and crushed under the worst bout of FOMO of her life, Vanesa unpacked her clothes and placed them in the drawers separated by outfit. She got her ski outerwear ready, wishing she'd gone with pink like she'd wanted to instead of boring black like Amber had insisted on. Hunter had chosen blue and yellow for his gear because of Rosario Central, Papi's favorite fútbol team from Argentina. At least he'd stand out in the snow.

Vanesa checked her phone, but there were no more

messages, only a notification that their class would start soon. She sprang into action. If they left the room early, she and Hunter could explore the lodge before class.

"Hunter," she said, shaking his arm. "We need to go."

His forehead was dotted with sweat, making his hair extra curly and his cheeks super flushed.

"So tired," he mumbled before turning to his side and making a pillow with his pudgy hands. The stuffed dog rolled off the bed, and Vanesa caught it before it fell. She left it there on the edge.

"We can't miss the class," she insisted, shaking his arm and trying to pull on it.

But Hunter wouldn't budge. Usually he had endless energy, but when he collapsed in exhaustion, there was no waking him. Mami complained that when he was a baby, nap conditions had to be perfect or he'd wake up in a murderous mood. Out of the house, it was another story. He could sleep through loud movies, dancing competitions, and even basketball games. When Hunter crashed after a sugar rush, the family could only wait it out.

Papi would be sad if they missed class, but most important, Vanesa didn't want to sit here watching videos of her friends having fun without her.

She considered her options. If she left, chances were good she'd be back before Hunter even realized she'd been gone. In that case, she'd be making her parents happy for not wasting the class, and she could *maybe* persuade them to make Hunter give her the bed. It would be fair.

She scribbled a note for her brother just in case.

Will be back soon. Stay here.

Vane

She kept it simple because he was only in second grade and his reading skills were still rusty, unlike hers. She wasn't Reader of the Year for four years in a row for nothing. This was reason eighteen for why she deserved the bed, and she filed it in her mind for future use in case she needed it.

She put on her snow pants and jacket and stuffed her gloves into her pockets.

"Hunter," she called one more time, her skin already prickling with sweat. It was toasty inside the room, but outside, she'd need all the layers she had on to keep warm. Hunter didn't reply, so she left the room quietly, like a shadow, taking one of the key cards with her.

The hallway was deserted, except for a room-service tray with scattered fries and a glob of ketchup visible under a napkin—yuck. She checked to make sure her room key was safe in her pocket, pushed the elevator button, and ran down the stairs to the lobby. Sending the elevator off by itself would be more fun with Hunter, but she still laughed.

She couldn't wait to see the other kids, especially Emma, and if she was being honest, even Beck. In spite of her attitude, Beck had a pull Vanesa couldn't resist.

Chapter Four
Annabeth Who?

To her surprise, the only people in the lobby were Beck and the concierge, Luís. Vanesa took a couple of deep breaths to compose herself. She had to up her game if she wanted to win her over.

Beck sat on a window seat with a book in her hand. She was dressed from head to toe in different shades of pink. She looked like a ski-themed Barbie, and Vanesa wished, again, that she'd chosen pink for her snow gear after all. Beck's golden hair cascaded over the side of her face, and though Vanesa couldn't see her expression, she felt the girl's attention on her.

Not knowing if she should approach Beck and try to make amends, Vanesa checked her phone. It always saved her from awkward situations. But the phone was suspiciously quiet. When there was no response to her question (*What are you guys up to?*), she paced back and forth near the fireplaces.

Every few seconds, she glanced over at the front desk. But Luís paid her no attention. He was on the phone, too—the landline—talking with what seemed like stranded guests.

"We'll be awaiting your arrival at any time, Mr. Smith. I hope you can make your next connection," he said. He dramatically rolled his eyes, which canceled out the cheery tone of his voice.

Vanesa smiled. Then she glanced back at the window seat. Beck was pretending she hadn't noticed Vanesa trying to make eye contact with her, but Vanesa noted the other girl hadn't turned a single page. Vanesa didn't want to be the first to break the heavy silence, so she studied the black-and-white portraits on the walls. She examined the woman with bushy brown hair and fiery eyes she had noticed earlier. In one of them, the woman posed next to a steam engine, surrounded by railroad workers. She held a large hammer in her hand, as though she'd single-handedly laid the rails. The date beneath the picture was 1899. Gosh! Hunter loved trains. He'd love to see these pictures. Hadn't Mami mentioned that a historical train still ran in nearby Heber City? Maybe they could make a quick visit to the train station, if she and Hunter wanted a break from skiing and her parents from spa treatments and catching up on TV shows. Maybe she could find out more about the woman.

Vanesa was so focused on the pictures that Luís startled her when he spoke.

"Annabeth Grant. She was a wonder woman." Luís's voice was awed instead of annoyed, like it had been moments ago.

Vanesa turned to look at him, and he pointed at a tiny plaque next to the entrance. She hadn't even noticed it before. It read:

ANNABETH GRANT (1870–1965). ADVENTURER, RANCHER, ATHLETE, AND SCHOLAR. KEEPER OF PINECLOUD, ITS INHABITANTS, AND ITS GUESTS.

A smile twinkled in Luís's eye. "Although she lived in another century, Annabeth is still our main attraction. She never really left us."

Chills ran over Vanesa's body. She wanted to ask him what he meant, but the phone rang again. Before he answered it, he motioned toward Beck and added, "Our guest Rebecca is reading a book about Annabeth. Maybe she could tell you more about her. Now talk quietly, please. I need to answer the phone."

Before Vanesa could reply that she and Beck—Rebecca?—weren't exactly on speaking terms, Luís was already reciting, "Pinecloud Lodge, how may I help you?" with all the wonder and admiration gone from his voice.

Gingerly, Vanesa glanced at the girl who sat on the window seat like a statue. A nagging voice in her head told her Beck was most likely waiting for her to apologize before she told her anything about Annabeth.

Vanesa wanted to mute that little voice like she muted the notifications from annoying apps that reminded her to brush her teeth or, even worse, put her phone down. She knew she had to take the first step, but she didn't want to.

Nobody in her family had to wonder where Hunter had learned to be so stubborn.

Finally, she made herself walk over to Beck. "I'm sorry I thought your mom was your grandma. That was rude of me." She'd also bumped into Beck and worn the same outfit as her, but thinking Beck's mom was her grandma was probably her worst offense, so she kept it at that.

Beck's nostrils flared, but when she finally looked at Vanesa, her eyes seemed very sad. Vanesa felt a twinge of sympathy. She, too, would be upset if anyone had made that mistake with her own mom. Right now, Beck didn't look like a celebrity.

Beck didn't say anything. Not *It's okay. It's a common mistake. Let's be friends now.*

She shrugged one shoulder like she didn't care about Vanesa's blunder, but judging by her pressed lips, Vanesa thought Beck cared very much.

Vanesa didn't know what to say to that, so she stayed silent. After a few awkward seconds that stretched on forever, she said, "Luís said you're reading about Annabeth Grant."

Would it be too much if she added that she loved reading, too? Or that she was also curious about Annabeth? Would Beck think she was copying her?

Beck's face softened, and her eyes had a look that might be described as *wistful* in a book. "She was an incredible woman," Beck said. "She didn't care about what anyone thought of her."

"Oh," Vanesa said, searching in her mind for something to add. "I . . . I don't care what anyone thinks of me, either, Rebecca."

Which was the greatest lie of all time. Of course she cared what others thought of her! That was all she cared about. She cared whether the Sunshine Darlings—mainly Amber—thought she was cool and wanted her in their club. Whether Mami and Papi thought she was a good daughter and sister. Whether Beck really thought she was an airhead like she'd called her earlier in the lobby.

Judging by the look on Beck's face, her opinion of Vanesa plummeted every time Vanesa opened her mouth.

Luckily, at that moment, a whiny sound broke the uncomfortable silence.

Vanesa looked over her shoulder and saw the enormous dog walking into the lobby. In spite of his whining, the dog seemed to be smiling. Vanesa wouldn't wrestle him to the ground or tickle him, but maybe she could see why Hunter had loved him immediately. She wished she wasn't terrified of him.

"Easy, Rocky," said a tall, skinny guy who didn't look a day older than fifteen. It was the boy who'd been salting the sidewalk earlier. He wore a green plaid vest like the other lodge employees and held a sign that said SKI CLASS in kindergarten-y handwriting. He looked too young to be working at the lodge, much less teaching a class. Maybe he was just guiding the kids to the slopes . . .

"Remember," the boy told the dog, "you need to stay still and quiet like a . . . rock." The boy laughed at his own joke, but his attention flittered to Luís, who was already eyeing the boy with a warning look. Luís placed a finger over his lips, and the boy mouthed, *"Sorry."*

"Excuse me . . . ," Vanesa said to the boy in the quietest voice ever. She glanced at his name tag: GEORGE. "George, is the ski class meeting here like it says on the schedule?"

The boy's face lit up. "Yes! Are you signed up?" he whispered loudly.

He looked at her with such an eager, kid-like expression, she was *sure* he was too young to be their instructor.

"Yes," she said. "My dad signed me up. I'm Vanesa Campos."

The boy looked down at his clipboard and said, "And Hunter? Rocky is here at his request."

Now Hunter would be sad for real.

"He's not coming," Vanesa said. "He fell asleep."

Seeing the boy's disappointed expression, she wondered if she should go back and wake her brother. But Hunter wouldn't be ready to wake up for a while.

Before she changed her mind, the boy clapped his hands, making her jump, and said, "Well, then! Are you in, too?" He was looking at Beck.

She nodded wordlessly and went back to the book without even telling him her name.

The boy sent Vanesa a look asking for clarification, but Vanesa didn't dare add anything that would make Beck think she was even more of an airhead.

He shrugged. "Let's wait a minute to see if anyone else turns up, but let's move away from the desk. We don't want to bother Luís."

The kids followed the boy away from the concierge toward a hallway. He led them to an entrance that looked like a mudroom, with benches and lockers. He continued, "Here we are. Luís won't hear us here . . . Anyway. Where was I?" He looked down at the clipboard. "Right! Yeah . . . there are two more names on my list. My name's Bryce, by the way; you probably thought it was George because of my badge." He pointed at his name tag and smiled. He had very straight teeth. The freckles on his face made him look even younger.

"Hi, Bryce. That's a nice name," Vanesa said, and when she realized she'd actually waved, she quickly put her hand down.

"Bryce like the canyon. Ever been there?"

Vanesa shook her head. Beck stood, arms crossed, tapping her foot and looking at Bryce as if she wondered when they'd get going. She kept her book under her arm.

But Bryce didn't seem to care. "George was promoted to snowboard instructor, so he won't be here until tomorrow, if he can make it, that is. I'm more of a classic sports guy. I mean, ski is easier to learn, but it takes a lifetime to master. On the other hand, snowboard is hard at the beginning, but then anyone can flip or twist in the air." He laughed sarcastically and looked from Beck to Vanesa, as if waiting for them to agree and laugh, too.

Vanesa smiled out of politeness, but Beck's face was like a clay mask.

At the lack of support, Bryce seemed to shrink. His vest hung loose on his shoulders. He explained, "The thing is, I'm double-tasking today, teaching the ski class *and* watching Rocky. Because of the storm, we're kind of short-staffed, you see?" His eyes flickered in the lobby's direction, and he stepped closer to Vanesa, as if he were about to reveal an ultra-special secret. He whispered, "Not that I told you we're understaffed, or that I'm not fully trained, okay?" Bryce ruffled Rocky's fur and said, "It's his first week on the job, too. We're kind of twins, wouldn't you say?"

Vanesa laughed nervously. The guy looked like a stick that Rocky would easily snap in two. Also, why was everyone obsessed with twins?

The sound of running feet made her look up in alarm. To her delight, it was the real twins, Emma and Eric.

"We couldn't find you!" Emma said as she hugged Vanesa like they were already best friends.

Vanesa exclaimed, "I'm so happy it's you!"

Beck snorted, and the two girls let go as if they'd been scolded. Beck inspected her nails with an annoying smirk on her face.

From next to the stairs, Eric sent Vanesa a tight smile, but by the way his jaw hardened when he looked at Emma, Vanesa suspected they'd been fighting.

Bryce looked down at his clipboard and said, "Are you the Richardson twins? I have you on the list."

Emma blushed. "Please, none of this twin business. I'm Emma, and he's Eric. Two different people, okay?" From her tone, it sounded like she couldn't, or wouldn't, give any more explanation.

Bryce raised his eyebrows and mouthed, *"Oh-kay . . ."*

Vanesa patted her new-almost-friend Emma's arm. She had no idea what this deal with being two different people was, but she was completely on Emma's side. Brothers could be the worst pain in the world.

"What are we waiting for?" Eric asked. His voice sounded choky. In the light streaming through the stained-glass window, Emma's brown eyes looked regretful.

Vanesa saw Beck studying Emma's expression, too, but when she blinked, Beck had looked away.

"Little man is right! What are we waiting for?" Bryce exclaimed. "Form a line by this bench. I have all your boots here in the locker."

Rocky didn't move from his spot in front of the lockers until Bryce snapped his fingers. The dog bolted to his feet and waited at attention, looking as excited as Vanesa felt.

Chapter Five
Twisted Tongues and Other Troubles

Vanesa didn't remember needing help putting her ski boots on when she was younger, but she let Bryce clasp the boot buckles. He pulled them tight as he warned, "If you do it wrong, your whole day can be ruined! Can't be too careful."

When they finally pushed open the door, the snow was so bright, the glare hurt Vanesa's eyes. She pulled her goggles down, and the world took on a yellowish tinge. A pity, because even through her squinted eyes, she'd seen that the cold made every tree and needle, every rock and snowdrift look sharper, more vivid. But she kept the goggles on, so at least she wouldn't go blind.

"Race you!" Emma challenged her and took off awkwardly toward the chairlift. The snow was deep, and it took a while to get used to walking with ski boots on. Also, the skis were heavy. Vanesa was panting after a few steps. Her dad had mentioned it could be harder to breathe up in the mountains, but she hadn't believed him until now. Even though her lungs hurt, she still laughed at the way Emma swung her legs to the sides so she could run.

Bryce saved her from running when he called Emma back. "We're meeting here first!" He pointed to a small slope, smaller than the one Vanesa had first skied on when she was seven years old. She hoped they were gathering only briefly to go over some rules. She gazed longingly at the high runs that cut through the mountain as if a giant had dropped a smooth white carpet down to the valley. She was eager for black diamond and double black diamond trails, not bunny slopes.

"Oh my gosh," she heard Beck muttering behind her. "Is it so hard to obey a few simple rules?"

"Emma's such a show-off!" Eric added, but he sounded jealous. He was way behind, too.

"I wasn't talking about your sister," Beck said in a harsh voice.

Vanesa stumbled as if Beck's words had pelted her on her back. She hadn't disobeyed at all! Beck and Eric snickered. Vanesa saw she was right underneath a signpost with green, blue, and black arrows. Trying to save face, she fumbled with her gloves and took a selfie, making sure the sign fit behind her in the frame. She circled the black sign that read WILD CHILD SLOPE and sent it to the Darlings, although if Mami saw her, she'd say that Vanesa was technically lying because she wasn't heading to the advanced slopes yet.

Feeling Beck's eyes on her, Vanesa's cheeks flamed. Beck seemed worried that Vanesa would get her in the picture, but Vanesa didn't want a picture with Beck anyway. She kept walking to where Bryce directed them, where the green arrow pointed at Green Deer Run, the baby slopes. She'd do as she was supposed to for now, but the first chance she got, she'd head out to the lifts for the fun, adrenaline-pumping slopes she'd been planning on forever.

At the sight of a fresh mound of powder, Vanesa had an idea.

"Finally!" she exclaimed. She dropped her skis, gloves, and helmet and plopped herself on the ground to make her first snow angel of this trip, the first one in forever. Sand angels at the beach didn't turn out the same.

The cold seeped through all the layers, and she shivered when her skin broke into goose bumps. She laughed, imagining the heat from being embarrassed leaving her in a swirl of steam. "I love this!" she exclaimed.

Vanesa clambered back up to look at her angel, trying not to ruin the outline. Next to her, Emma lay down on her back, waving her arms and legs like windshield wipers. She, too, got up to inspect her angel. Because she had a pointy hood on her jacket, it looked like the snow angel had a conehead. The girls laughed. Beck and Eric glowered at them.

"Kids! Attention!" Bryce called to them in what sounded like a fake voice, deep and serious, like he was trying to impress someone.

Vanesa looked around and saw why. One of the Grant brothers—he wore a coonskin hat, but she couldn't remember if that was Zachariah or Josiah—noticed her looking and waved. She waved back and ran to Bryce's side. Running in the snow was like running through thrashing waves. Vanesa realized it was basically the same thing, except this was frozen. How amazing the winter was! The only one who didn't have a hard time in the snow was Rocky. As if by magic, outside in the snow, his perfect habitat, he seemed more alert and not so flighty. He was bounding along effortlessly.

Bryce had led the kids to a clearing halfway between the main lodge and the older-looking cabin: the kids' lodge. Rocky sat obediently next to Bryce. A little mountain of equipment, including a pair of snowshoes and a walkie-talkie, lay next to a makeshift circle of logs. Maybe he'd need them for his next class.

"Welcome to skiing with Bryce and Rocky," Bryce said.

Beads of sweat exploded on Vanesa's forehead from the effort of walking through the snow. She loved the cooling sensation when a breeze dried the droplets. Her heart pounded, the excitement already running through her.

Emma's hood had slipped off, and thin rivulets of steam swirled from her head. Vanesa was grateful her beanie tied under her chin like a helmet. She wouldn't lose it.

"While I go over the basics, please put on your helmets,

then go ahead and clasp the right ski, and the right ski only, under your boot. You should hear a click." Bryce handed a pair of ski poles to each kid. While the four of them tried to clip their boots onto the skis, he continued as though he'd memorized a speech. "Like I was saying before, snowboarding looks cool in videos and stuff, but skiing is classy. It's the king of sports. It's intuitive and a great workout!"

"You can say that again," Emma blurted out, and mimicked wiping the sweat off her forehead. Vanesa smiled, but Eric and Beck looked like they'd eaten lemons.

Bryce gave Emma a quick smile but continued with the class. "All right, let's balance on one foot along this stretch of trail."

He looked at Rocky as if expecting the dog to give him a thumbs-up. Vanesa was the first to take off. This was the easiest thing in the world. She didn't even need the poles to balance herself on one foot. The butterflies in her stomach made her giddy. She was ready for the real thing. She already knew all this stuff for babies.

Babies.

Hunter totally needed this lesson. Not her. She glanced toward the lodge. She couldn't tell which window was her room, and she wished that she'd tried a little harder to wake up her brother. Maybe Bryce could give him a private lesson later today or tomorrow.

She waited at the other end of the practice trail for the other kids. Noticing she'd already clasped the other ski on, Bryce winked at her.

"You're a quick learner," he said, and the warmth in Vanesa's chest was like a growing balloon of pride. "But don't be overconfident."

His words punctured the balloon instantly. When Bryce gave them the go-ahead to glide in the opposite direction, she made sure she wasn't the first one. This gave her the chance to notice that even though Emma was daring, she was wobbly on her feet. Eric looked so tense, Vanesa's shoulders hurt in sympathy. And Beck advanced in perfect form, but slow like a snail.

Not able to hold in her enthusiasm anymore, Vanesa propelled herself with the poles and slid past Beck. But she miscalculated the gap between Beck and the edge of the trail and bumped the girl, who lost her balance.

Vanesa heard the thump of a body falling on the packed snow and a loud "Ow! Why would you do that, Vanesa!"

Vanesa turned at full speed, mortified that she'd made Beck fall and, at the same time, absolutely thrilled that her body still remembered how to do a perfect wedge turn.

"Sorry," she said, but no one seemed to hear.

Beck tried to get up, but her skis tangled beneath her. Vanesa thought that maybe the skis were too long for her, but she didn't want to make things worse, so she stayed silent. She glided back to the small huddle of kids, but stayed outside the circle.

"Nothing's broken, right?" Bryce asked Beck, a look of absolute worry on his face. He coached her through getting her skis parallel so she could get up while Rocky whined and pranced around Beck as though he could help.

Beck's eyes were brimming with tears by the time she came over to the group. She was so pale, it was a good thing she wore such bright colors. Otherwise, she'd be lost in the snow. Vanesa bit her lip so she wouldn't blurt out such a tasteless comment in the moment.

"I think I'm okay," Beck finally said. "My shin hurts a lot, though."

Bryce scratched his head, like he was trying to figure out a puzzle. "Maybe your tongue is twisted."

Beck's cheeks turned bright red when the other kids burst into laughter.

"My tongue?" she asked, outraged.

Now it was Bryce who was embarrassed. "Sorry. The boot's tongue. Maybe it's twisted inside and it's constricting your leg unnecessarily."

He started unclasping Beck's boot. Vanesa sighed loudly. She didn't want to be stuck here on the baby trail all day. The sun was sinking rapidly.

"Bryce?" Vanesa said. "Can I slide down that hill over there? I'll be careful."

Bryce was struggling with the buckle on Beck's boot that wouldn't come off. "It's too cold," he muttered.

By then, Emma had joined Vanesa. Eric stood next to Beck, helping her balance while Bryce fixed her boot.

"Bryce?" Vanesa insisted. "Just one run down that hill, please?"

Bryce puffed. Steam came out of his nose. Finally, he nodded.

"Just a run down the hill and that's it, okay?"

He sounded like Mami when she was busy with something and gave in only so that Vanesa would stop pestering her. Vanesa didn't wait for Bryce to change his mind. She quickly turned and headed to the hill, Emma next to her.

Chapter Six
Winter Is Coming

Vanesa reached the top of the bunny slope and waited for Emma. The other girl seemed as excited as she was but kept glancing down to where Eric balanced on one foot around the small circle where Bryce still struggled with Beck's boot.

"Maybe the boot got busted when she fell?" Emma wondered aloud.

A heavy feeling fell in Vanesa's stomach. What if the boot got busted because of *her* and now Beck couldn't ski? On the other hand, maybe it would be for the better. Beck looked like she'd rather be back inside. Eric didn't look happy, either. He kept glancing at Emma as if silently asking for attention.

The two girls slid gently down the small hill, and Emma gave a *whoop*. Vanesa grinned as she made it to the bottom, knowing she was ready for more than the baby slopes. At the same time, they noticed the chairlift to the blue-level slope, the intermediate one, was within reach.

"Let's try the blue slope!" Emma said as though she'd read Vanesa's mind.

"Yes!" Vanesa exclaimed. But then she looked toward the lodge. Her little brother was still asleep in the room and her parents were in the spa, thinking she was taking care of him. She turned and looked behind her at Bryce, Beck, and Eric. The three of them were doing boring runs down the trail with Rocky trotting beside them.

"Just one turn," Emma said, pulling her by the arm. "We'll be okay."

"All right," Vanesa replied, and followed Emma.

There was no line for the lift, and the attendant helped Emma get on the chair, but Vanesa felt like she'd been born for this, for winter. She hopped and sat just as the attendant girl let go of the chair, which quickly lifted into the air.

From below, the lift didn't seem too long, but it gained speed quickly. Vanesa's boots felt heavy as gravity pulled her down while the chair soared above the trees. A gray cloud loomed over the mountain—Little Bald.

"Yikes! We're so high up!" Emma exclaimed, clutching Vanesa's arm.

Vanesa laughed nervously. She took her phone out of her pocket and snapped a picture of the view, but she didn't dare send it and risk missing their stop. Carefully, she put the phone back in her pocket.

"Wow!" she gasped, looking at the valley below her feet. "This is beautiful!"

From this height, she could see the entire main lodge and the roof of the kids' lodge. They were separated by the clearing with the circle of logs and, she could see now, a big pool covered with a tarp. There was also an ice-skating rink and a volleyball net that had been abandoned in the snow. Steam rose from a Jacuzzi next to the kids' area. She would try that tonight and maybe get her parents to join her. She thought she saw Bryce waving his arms, calling to the girls, but she couldn't be sure. Forest surrounded the Pinecloud complex, and enormous birds she'd never seen before—eagles?— glided below the clouds.

"Come on!" Emma exclaimed, and jumped off the chair before Vanesa had time to react. This was their stop.

Vanesa kicked her feet as she tried to shimmy out of the lift. One of her skis unlatched from her boot as she flailed, and Emma had to slide out of the way so it wouldn't land on her.

The chair was already lifting.

"Jump, Vanesa!" Emma screamed from behind her. She looked so far away on the ground.

Vanesa felt like time froze as she considered what to do. She could go to the next stop, but it was for a scarier run, for much more experienced skiers. If she tried to ski down the mountain, she could get seriously hurt. Then the family vacation would be totally ruined. Why hadn't she stayed on the beginners' hill?

No. She couldn't ride up to the black diamond trail. She had to jump. Now. Time sped up again.

She closed her eyes and let herself fall.

She landed with a hollow sound, but because of the one remaining ski, she couldn't roll to the side to protect herself. A sharp pain ran up her leg as if there was an electrical current parallel to her bones.

"Get out of the way!" a ski lift attendant called.

Vanesa looked up. The next seat in the lift approached with two young men who barely avoided hitting her as they jumped out.

"I'm going to complain to the manager," one of the men said. He had an accent but not like Mami's and Papi's. "All these unsupervised children, making it unsafe for the rest of us!"

They zipped down the slope in the blink of an eye.

Emma glided toward Vanesa. "Are you okay?" She looked worried.

Vanesa nodded, getting to her feet. Now her attention was fully on the ski slope ahead of her. It was only the blue run, the intermediate. But it looked so steep from up here!

"The only way to go is down," she said.

Emma looked scared, too. "It won't be so bad. Let's go," she said, and even if she didn't have perfect form—her skis were too far apart—she looked confident on her feet.

Vanesa, though, struggled to get her ski to click back on her boot. She stomped on it, and it clicked in precariously. Her leg throbbed in pain.

A snowflake fell on her nose. The dark clouds were moving toward the resort at full speed. A voice inside told her she better follow Emma and join the rest of the group.

This was what she'd wanted, wasn't it? She squared her skis and looked down the hill.

She could see a purple blur with braids flying in all directions as Emma made it to the bottom and turned to call for Vanesa. The other three figures seemed like statues, arms crossed and backs straight. She couldn't see their faces from this distance, but she was sure Bryce, Beck, and Eric were scowling at her.

If Emma could make it down, then she could, too. She must.

How long had Vanesa been gone now? How long had she left Hunter on his own?

She tested her boot once more, unsure it would stay clasped, and pushed off.

Her skis slid smoothly over the packed snow, and she concentrated hard on keeping them pointed straight. She loved the wind whipping on her face. She licked her lips. They burned because the air was dry. She hoped Mami had brought lip balm to share. She tucked her poles under her arms as she hurtled down the hill, gaining speed. Just as she was thinking she'd make it, one foot slid out to the side and suddenly she was skidding in a cloud of snow. She stopped, landing on her butt, just in front of the other kids, her one ski thrown to the side.

She mentally checked her body, found nothing hurt—and a smile stretched from ear to ear. Her fall might not have been glamorous, but she'd felt like she was flying.

The happiness didn't last long.

"What in the world were you thinking?" Bryce exclaimed once he made sure she was safe and sound.

The smiles slipped off Vanesa's and Emma's faces.

Bryce sounded way older than the freckly, awkward boy from a couple of hours before.

"I'm sorry," Vanesa said for the second time in the day.

Beck scoffed and whipped her hair dramatically. She held her helmet in her hand.

"This adventure of yours was only fun for you two," Bryce said. "It's not fair for Eric and Beck to wait while you make it down the mountain. Tomorrow, everyone will have to follow the rules, or I'll have a word with your parents."

Rocky barked as if to say *amen* or *well said*.

Emma and Eric argued in loud whispers.

"You always leave me behind," Eric was muttering, and Emma, pouting, pretended not to hear. Vanesa caught Beck's gaze, and the older girl rolled her eyes.

The snowflakes fell thicker and faster now. One fell right in Vanesa's eye as she was taking off her goggles.

She looked up and realized the dark gray cloud that had looked far, far away when they'd first walked out to practice was now completely on top of the lodge. It extended all the way down to the valley, like the storm was here to stay. If she were Chicken Little, she'd say the sky was falling one snowflake at a time. This would be the most wintry vacation ever.

Bryce, too, gazed up, and in an ominous voice, he announced, "Winter is coming."

In spite of the awkwardness of being told off in front of everyone, Vanesa couldn't help it. She broke into laughter. What was Bryce talking about? Winter was all around them! Josiah had said the snow had been light this winter, but snow covered the roofs of both buildings. If she tried to dig a hole to find the ground, she'd have to shovel through several feet of snow to finally scrape dead grass.

"Never mind," Bryce said. "But pay attention, kids. At this high altitude, the weather can change in minutes. One moment you're covering your eyes from the glare of the sun, and the next it's snowing so hard you can't see two feet ahead."

Vanesa looked around in alarm. He had to be exaggerating, just as he'd overreacted about how long they'd had to wait for Vanesa and Emma to ski down from the blue slope. This was only a sprinkling.

Emma looked at Vanesa and rolled her eyes.

Bryce looked like he wanted to make sure the girls understood he meant business. "No, seriously. You need to pay attention to this. When there's a blizzard, even if you're a few feet from each other, you won't be able to hear your own voice. Even if you yell. The snow absorbs all sound. That's why we bring Rocky along. He can hear through any blizzard, but by the time he finds you, it might be too late." He made a gesture across his own throat.

Rocky was pouncing at invisible enemies on the snow. His attention span had reached its limit. Vanesa doubted that in an emergency he'd be able to focus enough to find anyone, much less save a life.

"If he's too late to find us, we might be dead?" Emma asked. There was a bit of fear in her voice now.

"Or you might lose limbs to frostbite. Cold is very powerful."

Eric and Beck walked ahead as Emma and Vanesa unstrapped the bindings of their skis.

"Where do we leave our gear?" Vanesa asked, trying to compensate for running off earlier.

Beck was unimpressed, but Bryce's face softened.

"I can take most of it back," Bryce said. "You'll have to wait a few minutes before you take your boots off because they're so cold. Then you can leave them inside the mudroom. Now go along back to the main lodge. See you later."

"At the kids' lodge?" asked Vanesa. She was ready for the big-screen movie night the schedule had promised.

Bryce shook his head. "You know what? I don't like this storm. Let's meet in the lobby first, right after dinner. If the storm continues like this, we might have to improvise, like in the old days before the renovations. It might be too dangerous to go out tonight."

Emma and Vanesa looked at each other, disappointed. Surely the storm wouldn't be that bad, right?

Without another word, Bryce collected the equipment and began piling it on a sleigh while Rocky pranced around him, eating the snow. Vanesa looked out at the kids' lodge, where a plume of smoke rose from its chimney. She imagined inside would be like the cabin from the Little House on the Prairie stories Hunter loved.

She'd have to warn her scatterbrained brother about this storm. If it was too dangerous to even cross to the other building, then this storm was serious. The wind had a bite that hadn't been so sharp before. Vanesa shivered. She also had to warn Hunter about the blue slope. It was way worse than it looked.

"S'mores and hot chocolate?" Emma asked, breathing hard as they made their way to the lodge. "It says on the schedule it's in the back room."

S'mores! How could Vanesa have forgotten?

"Of course!" she said, her mouth watering with the promise of butterscotch marshmallows.

Beyond a big set of French doors, the air was toasty inside the foyer. Eric's and Beck's boots lay in a puddle. Vanesa looked back outside where the snow was gently falling.

"It's snowing! It's snowing," she chanted. "It never snows where I live. What about where you live?" she asked Emma.

Emma shook her head and laughed. "We live in Phoenix, Arizona. No snow for us."

Vanesa took out her phone, and her surprise at what she saw almost made her drop it. It wasn't the lack of messages from the Darlings. But the time.

It was almost four in the afternoon, and she'd left her brother right after one!

"Oh no!" she exclaimed. "I can't do s'mores right now. I need to get my brother first." She fought with the boots until her feet were free. Without the pressure of the boot, her foot hurt even more.

But she had to make sure her brother was okay.

Emma made a face, and Vanesa worried that she'd offended her new friend. "What?" she asked.

"I have to get my brother, too, before he goes to my parents with the gossip."

Right! Vanesa's parents could find out about her recklessness from other people. It would be a miracle if they didn't hear she'd gone on the blue slope without permission. Emma looked as worried as Vanesa felt, so she asked, "Is your brother always in such a bad mood with you?"

"It's our birthday tomorrow," she said.

"Happy birthday!" Vanesa said, and patted her new friend on the shoulder.

Emma smiled, but she had a conflicted expression on her face. "We were born in Boston at two a.m. Eastern Time, which will be midnight here. We have a tradition of staying up to celebrate right at two a.m. Eastern Time, and we can't agree on how we want to do it this year. He's been mad at me ever since I suggested a . . ." Her words trailed off.

"A what?" Vanesa asked, failing to imagine what could've made Eric so mad at Emma.

Emma spoke quickly, almost as if she were embarrassed, "I want a piñata, and he doesn't because he says we're too old for that kind of thing. But I love piñatas, and . . . yeah . . . I told him I was sick and tired of him and that maybe we should stop doing things together. I feel bad about it now. Kind of."

Vanesa felt a twinge of regret. She wouldn't acknowledge it aloud to Emma (what would she think?), but she'd said the same words to her baby brother, and all because he'd claimed the bed before she did.

She hoped he was still asleep, but he never napped for three hours.

"Brothers are a pain," Vanesa said, "but at least we're not alone like Beck. Maybe that's why she's so angry all the time."

Emma's eyes flashed. "Not exactly. She and Eric spent the whole time together. She wasn't alone."

Vanesa would be terribly jealous if Hunter spent all his time with a stranger—a stranger who didn't like Vanesa, for some reason Vanesa couldn't understand.

"Anyway, see you in a bit!" Emma said. "If not for s'mores, I'll meet you at the kids' lodge. Can you imagine? A place just for us!"

Vanesa got excited again. She had to get Hunter, then she could enjoy her time.

"See you later!" she called, waving at Emma.

Vanesa headed to her room, anxious to get out of her snow pants and check her texts again. After making sure Hunter was okay, of course. Had her phone been out of range while she skied? Otherwise, why weren't the Darlings replying to her last message?

Chapter Seven
Bunny Slippers Can't Fix Everything

Vanesa ran into the room she shared with Hunter, totally expecting him to be awake. Hopefully, he'd be watching his ninja show on TV, ready to finally have some fun with her. And hopefully he'd forgotten their fight and decided to give her the bed, anyway. Because he was little, sometimes his interests and anger didn't last long.

She heard her parents talking in Spanish in the room across the hallway. Mami laughed. It sounded like the hot-stone massage had helped them relax after all. The vacation was already paying off. Mami better not hear about the mishap on the blue slope or about Vanesa leaving Hunter unwatched for so long, or else . . .

Vanesa opened the door and said, "Are you up, sleepyhead?"

No one responded. She ran to the bed and patted the ruffled covers. Maybe Hunter was still asleep, tangled in the comforter.

But Hunter wasn't there.

"Hunter," Vanesa called, trying to keep the growing fear out of her voice. She peeked in the bathroom. "Are you here?"

The bathroom smelled of fresh paint and wood shavings. She couldn't wait to soak in a bubble bath while gazing at the falling snow through the window. And by now, the snow was really falling.

A perfect snowflake clung to the glass window like a rebel instead of joining its friends gathering on top of the bushes, the windowsills, and every surface. Vanesa looked at it, mesmerized. It had an actual, perfect little snowflake shape! She'd always thought the way people drew holiday snowflakes was like when they drew Valentine's Day hearts. The human heart looks nothing like the emoji one. But this snowflake! It was breathtakingly beautiful.

She snapped a picture and sent it to the Darlings. They had to love this shot. The snowflake was a tiny miracle caught on her screen.

And outside, there were millions more! She was just starting to warm up after spending so much time in the snow, but she couldn't wait to get out there and enjoy it. She'd never get enough of it.

But she had to find Hunter first. Although it was still the afternoon, it had turned darker outside because of the storm. Vanesa's stomach rumbled, reminding her that she'd never had lunch.

Lunch!

Maybe Hunter had woken up hungry and gone to their parents' room to get room service. She hadn't heard his voice, but he could have been quiet, eating or playing *DragonVille* on Mami's phone.

Hopefully Mami wouldn't be upset that Hunter had been on his own when he slept. But what was Vanesa supposed to have done—miss the class?

But maybe, if she had stayed, she wouldn't have hurt Beck, gotten in trouble with Bryce, hurt herself . . .

She changed out of her cold snow pants and draped them over the bathtub to dry. She found a pair of comfy fleece pants and fluffy bunny slippers. When she caught a look at herself in the wall-to-wall mirror, she took a selfie and sent it to the Sunshine Darlings. They hadn't replied to the snowflake, but Amber wasn't a nature lover. The slippers were adorable, though. They had to reply to this one, right? They hadn't sent a single message for a couple of hours, which was super suspicious. Had something bad happened to them? They had to reply eventually. Vanesa wasn't the only one who had to maintain the streak.

Imagining the Darlings drenched in rain, Vanesa crossed the hallway to her parents' room and knocked on the door.

Mami was still laughing when she opened the door. "Hi, mi amor. How was your day? You got suntanned! Your nose looks flechada."

Vanesa brushed her face with her hand. The skin on her nose did feel tingly. When she took the selfie, she hadn't noticed that she looked red, but a quick glance in the mirror next to the door showed her that, like Mami said, the sun had painted her face with an arrow of light. The lighting in this room was better.

"Next time remember to wear sunscreen out in the snow. And make sure Hunter puts it on, too, okay?"

Vanesa had more pressing matters on her mind than the condition of her skin. Where was Hunter? She surveyed the room. It was identical to the one she shared with her brother, except there was a wonderful balcony, which looked empty. There was no sign of Hunter or Papi.

"Where's Papi?" she asked, playing it safe. No need to alert Mami so soon. Maybe Hunter was with Papi, sharing some father-son bonding time. But then, who had Mami been talking to?

Mami motioned with a nod. "In the bathroom."

"And Hunter? Is he with him?"

Mami chuckled, but her eyes narrowed. "Hunter? Of course he's not in the bathroom with Papi."

"Oh no!" Vanesa groaned. What if he'd gone out looking for her? In that case, what was she doing here, taking selfies and chitchatting with Mami? What if Hunter had gone skiing on his own? She had to find him.

Mami's smile vanished like she could see the catastrophic images in Vanesa's mind. "Where is your brother, Vanesa?"

Maybe she should've checked her own room better. Vanesa turned and went back across the hallway, her mom trailing her closely. Vanesa patted the covers again. She even looked under the bed and under the half-made sofa bed. She found only candy wrappers.

She followed the trail of wrappers all the way to the mini-fridge. She opened it with dread, and as the wrappers hinted, it seemed that Hunter had gone on another sugar binge. At the lodge, each little packet of candy in the mini-bar cost more than a bulk-size bucket back home! Her allowance was definitely not enough to cover this unexpected expense. What was Mami going to say?

"Vanesa!" Mami's voice snapped. "What is going on?"

Vanesa whipped around. By now, Papi was standing next to Mami, both of them with crossed arms and cross expressions.

"I'm sorry," Vanesa said.

"Where's Hunter?" Papi asked. By the way his eyebrows disappeared into his hair, she could tell he was making an effort not to panic. Yet.

"He fell asleep right before ski class, and—"

"You missed the class?" he interrupted.

Vanesa's phone vibrated in her pocket. Why did the Sunshine Darlings have to message her now? She couldn't look down in the middle of the argument.

"No!" Vanesa exclaimed, sounding way sharper than she had intended. "I didn't miss the class, Papi."

A look from her mom told her she was stretching her luck. She took a calming breath. The phone kept dancing in her pocket, sounding like a swarm of angry yellow jackets.

"Disculpa, Papi," Vanesa apologized. "What I mean is that I didn't miss the class. Hunter was in one of his sugar-low naps, and I decided to go, anyway."

"You left him alone?" Mami exclaimed, and tsked. "Hija, you had *one* job. One!"

Vanesa stayed quiet because Hunter's being alone wasn't even the worst of it. For all her determination not to ruin their family vacation, she'd made the greatest mistake ever. She'd lost her brother. No matter what she said to explain, Vanesa knew she'd be in trouble.

She had the best intentions, but the truth was that Hunter was missing.

"Where is he now?" Papi asked.

"I don't know," Vanesa said.

"Ay, Vane!" Mami exclaimed. "Did you at least look for him? Remember, bring me solutions, not problems!"

Vanesa tried to defend herself. "That's what I was trying to do! I was looking for him—"

"But why did you leave him?" Mami asked.

"I tried to wake him at least twice, and . . ." Vanesa remembered the note she'd written to her brother and looked at the desk. The note wasn't there. "I left a note! Look, it's not here." The stuffed dog was also gone.

She felt vindicated, but her parents didn't look so sure. Hunter's inhaler was right there next to the remote. He didn't always need it, but he *had* to carry it at all times just in case.

"Maybe he went looking for us in the spa?" Mami asked softly. "This place isn't big. Someone must have seen him."

Papi nodded and said, "I'll go check! You stay in the room in case he comes back."

"I'll go check the lobby!" Vanesa said.

Maybe Hunter had found the other kids and was eating s'mores while the whole family was needlessly panicking.

She turned around, pulling the phone out of her pocket to check the messages. She had four! But before she could open them, Mami's hand clamped on her shoulder.

"No phone, señorita. Venga para acá," Mami said, pointing back into the room.

Now Vanesa was really in trouble. When her mom went all formal in Spanish, it was never good news.

"But, Mami!" Vanesa complained, her heart revving as if she'd been trudging up a mountain. "I need the phone to communicate with you in case I find him."

Mami shook her head. "I just said the lodge isn't that big. You can come back and tell me whatever you need to say in person." She stretched out her hand, palm up, and waited. She didn't count. But Vanesa knew she only had seconds to come up with a plan.

Vanesa considered crying, begging, promising anything, but it was clear these tactics wouldn't work. She could try reasoning with Mami, though. Like Mami said, *hablando se entiende la gente*—when tears and whining didn't help, words could work miracles. By speaking, people understood one another.

"The thing is, I need the phone." Vanesa pressed the phone against her chest like a talisman.

Mami took a big breath. "Whatever for? You can find me or Papi easily. There are phones in every landing next to the escalators."

Those phones didn't text or take pictures, so they were out of the question. Vanesa decided to tell the truth. "I can't lose my streak. The Darlings have a one-hundred-and-sixteen-day streak. I need my phone with me."

Mami's eyes narrowed as she let out a sharp breath. "Are we really talking about streaks when your brother is lost?"

Vanesa looked down at her slippers. Not even the cute bunnies could cheer her up. Mami was right. What kind of sister was she? But she had to think of her future at school, too. If she blew this streak, the Darlings would kick her out of the group, and then she'd be friendless. The first half of seventh grade had already been hard, and that was with the Darlings' protection. Vanesa didn't dare think of facing the gigantic middle school building with hundreds of students on her own, or worse, with the Darlings against her.

"Mami, I promise I'll look for him and I'll never disappoint you again. I won't leave his side at all. Just don't take the phone."

Vanesa looked up at her mom. Despair must have been painted on her face because Mami's eyes softened. While Vanesa's heart fluttered with hope, Mami put her hand out again, shattering any illusion of ending seventh grade on a happy note. "Streaks reset at midnight. You have plenty of time to keep up with the silly streaks before then."

"They're not silly, Mami!" Vanesa didn't intend to shout. She clasped a hand over her mouth, but it was too late.

Now she'd ruined everything.

"I'm not an unreasonable person," Mami said. "Let's find Hunter and then we'll reconsider."

By *we*, she meant Papi and her. There went Vanesa's hopes of appealing to her dad for help. The longer she took to find Hunter, the longer she'd be phone-less—and friendless.

Vanesa turned her phone in and said, "I promise I'll find him, Mami, and you'll see I was trying my best."

Mami shook her head, disappointed. "Trying your best isn't always enough, Vane. You promised you'd behave this time around, and here we are. Now Hunter's missing."

Vanesa swallowed the knot that had formed in her throat.

"You're not going to cry because of your phone, are you?" Mami asked.

Even if it hurt, Vanesa swallowed the lump and said, "Of course not! It's just the dry air," and ran toward the stairs before her mom could call her back. She was sad about the phone situation, but she wasn't heartless. She had disappointed Mami. If trying didn't matter, then she was already failing at everything.

Chapter Eight
Yellow Jacket Alert

There was no time for elevators. Vanesa would find Hunter, and then Mami would see she'd been wrong.

Vanesa ran so fast, she almost bumped into Beck, who was coming up the stairs with her nose buried in a book again.

"Watch it!" Beck said.

Vanesa flinched, then took a long breath. Maybe Beck had seen Hunter.

"I . . . I . . . Sorry! Have you seen my brother?"

Beck looked taken aback.

"Sorry," Vanesa said, gulping air. "He's lost."

"He's lost or you lost him?" Beck asked.

Vanesa gritted her teeth, but she didn't have time to explain. "I think he went out looking for me, and there's a snowstorm coming."

Beck lowered her book and said, "I saw him going outside. With Eric."

Outside? In this weather? Did he even have his jacket on? Vanesa couldn't remember if she'd seen it in the room. Now she really was in trouble.

"But you told them we were done with the ski lesson, right?" Vanesa demanded. "You heard what Bryce said about the storm"

Beck blushed all the way to the tips of her blond hair. "I'm sorry," she said. "I didn't think to say anything."

Vanesa couldn't believe the girl could be so oblivious. "You can say that again—you didn't think."

Beck looked hurt and angry, but Vanesa didn't care that she was being unfair. Her problem could've been solved already if Beck had stopped the boys.

At the sound of running feet, both girls looked up. Emma was practically flying down the stairs. Her feet didn't seem to touch the paisley carpet that covered the steps.

"Watch it!" Beck and Vanesa yelled at the same time, but Beck suffered the brunt of the collision.

Emma leaned against the wall, rubbing her forehead and blinking very quickly, as if she was trying not to cry. The blinking wasn't working, and she must have known it because she finally pressed a hand over her face to hide her pain.

"Are you guys okay?" Vanesa asked Emma and Beck.

"What kind of airhead question is that?" Beck said, rubbing her shoulder. "Of course I'm not okay!"

A millisecond ago, Vanesa would've given Beck a hug to make her feel better, but now she wanted to delete her from her life. Why did she have to be so mean?

"I'd rather be an airhead than a human porcupine," Vanesa snapped. She tried to grasp at something else to say, but her heart was hammering so hard she couldn't concentrate. No doubt the words would come to her tongue later, when it was too late for a comeback.

Beck laughed, but her eyes were too shiny. "I'd rather be a human porcupine than a show-off!"

"At least I know how to do something other than read," Vanesa snapped, and the words seemed to have found a mark.

Vanesa didn't know why she said it—she liked to read, too. But seeing the smirk melt off Beck's face encouraged her a little. Beck didn't even know her. What gave her the right to judge her like this?

Vanesa was about to redouble her attack when Emma groaned.

Instead, Vanesa stepped closer to Emma and placed a hand on her shoulder. "Let me see."

Emma lowered her hand. She had a pink bump on her forehead that didn't look very serious but must have hurt.

"What in the world, guys?" Emma asked, her voice wobbly. She cleared her throat and continued, "Why were you standing in the middle of the stairs?"

Beck narrowed her eyes and shot back, "Why were *you* running down the stairs like zombies were chasing you? I bumped my head against the wall really hard, you know? What if we both went tumbling down? What if you hurt someone else?" At the last words, she glared at Vanesa and rubbed her hip where she'd gotten hurt when she fell in the snow. When Vanesa made her fall.

Emma's cheeks turned pink with embarrassment, but Vanesa didn't feel bad about bumping into Beck on the slopes anymore.

"Sorry about hitting you. It was an accident," Emma said. Beck looked like she was going to protest, so Emma put up a hand and added, "You're right, okay? I shouldn't have been running, but . . . but Eric got mad at me again, and . . . and he's missing, and I looked everywhere, but I can't find him!"

If Eric was missing as well, that could mean he and Hunter were together, like Beck had said.

When Vanesa looked at her, Beck pressed her lips hard and lifted her chin, challenging anyone to come at her with an accusation. Vanesa balled her fists tightly, but thinking of her brother, she exhaled and her thoughts cleared. She didn't have time for a fight with Beck right now. She'd get back at her later. She wanted to find her brother safe and sound, go back to their room, and have a cozy night.

Beck's eyes flittered toward the side, like she was thinking of making a run for it, but Emma was leaning against the wall, blocking her escape. Vanesa stood her ground on the staircase. Why had she ever wanted Beck to like her? Beck was ruining everything with her attitude.

Hands on her hips, Vanesa looked Beck straight in the eye and said, "Why couldn't you do the decent thing, Beck? I'm sorry I offended you, but I apologized! Besides, my brother is only seven years old. What did he ever do to you? Why didn't you remind Eric of what Bryce said?"

Emma stepped toward Beck. "Wait. You saw Eric and Vanesa's brother go out and you didn't tell them not to? Who *does* that?"

Beck was breathing fast. A shadow passed over her eyes, and the blush on her cheeks and the look of defiance on her face vanished. But Vanesa wouldn't give in.

"Where did they go?" she asked.

Beck swallowed as if telling the truth were the hardest thing she'd had to do in her life.

"Come on!" Emma urged. The beads in her hair clinked when she shook her head. "We should ask someone to help us! The snow is really coming down now. We can't waste any time."

The three girls looked at the window. The snow was falling faster than it had when Vanesa was up in her room. The wind blew, clumping the snowflakes into a solid sheet of white that blocked all color. Still, in the distance, a flickering light and a shock of yellow flashed like fairy lights.

A flickering light like that of a lantern.

Yellow like Hunter's jacket.

"What's that?" Vanesa asked, her senses sharpening. She moved next to the window and cupped her hand against the glass to see outside. There was the light, and a yellow . . . *something* moving toward it, near a tall post. It was the slope signpost, by the circle of logs where they'd had the orientation with Bryce before the ski class earlier today. Had it really been today? She checked her watch. It seemed like days had passed instead of only an hour.

"That's the old lodge, what they call the kids' lodge now," Beck said, squinting her eyes through the storm. "There's a light in the top floor of the building. If the kids' activities are canceled for the night, then who's there?"

Emma pulled on Vanesa's hand and said, "Maybe the boys headed up there, anyway. We need to go check."

Vanesa's heart pounded in her ears again. If Hunter was out there, she needed to go find him. Mr. Trouble had a lot of things to answer for.

Vanesa looked down and realized she was still wearing her fluffy slippers. In the hurry to do as her mom said, she hadn't thought to put her shoes back on.

As if she'd read Vanesa's mind, Emma pointed at her own feet and said, "Yikes. I didn't expect to go out, either." She was wearing slippers, too, although hers were lambs'-wool-lined booties. Beck, on the other hand, had running sneakers on, not ideal for the snow, either.

"Our boots might still be in the mudroom!" Vanesa exclaimed.

"What are we waiting for?" Emma asked.

Vanesa dashed after Emma, but Beck stopped her, pulling her by her shirt. Vanesa wanted to shake her off. Beck didn't understand their urgency because she didn't have a brother who might be in danger.

Beck said, "Listen, what if we cross to the kids' lodge and they aren't even there? First we need to figure out if it's really them."

Vanesa didn't need to make sure. She wanted to rush out, but Emma said, "Good thinking."

The fight went out of Vanesa like a breath.

"Beck, tell us where you saw them last," Emma said. "What door did they leave through?"

Beck sighed but seemed to understand how important this was to Vanesa and Emma. "Follow me," she said. "It was just a few minutes ago." She led Emma and Vanesa downstairs, holding on to the railing.

They passed the lobby, and Luís, who was again on the phone, shot them a tight smile. Without any other prompting, the three girls exchanged a look and continued on. There was no way they could tell Luís what was happening, that the two boys were missing. He was busy redirecting stranded guests, and they didn't have time to wait until he was done with the call.

In the back of her mind, a nagging little voice told Vanesa to go tell her parents—right now—that she thought Hunter had gone to the kids' lodge in the middle of a blizzard. But another voice that sounded like Mami spoke louder in her mind: *Vanesa, don't bring me problems. Bring me solutions.*

Last Thanksgiving, when Vanesa had turned twelve, they'd celebrated her birthday at the trampoline place against her parents' better judgment. The holiday weekend had turned the trampoline place into a zoo, but Amber had insisted, and Vanesa couldn't let her friend down. Amber wanted the trampoline place and accepted no compromises.

Now, as she rushed down the stairs, Vanesa realized she'd made the same mistake as she had on her birthday: She had left her brother alone. Now his life might be in danger. She couldn't repeat the past.

There was no way she could return to the room without him.

She followed Beck toward a side door she hadn't noticed before.

As soon as Beck opened the door, the cold from outside ate up the warmth from the heater vent that enveloped the hallway. They hadn't even stepped out the door, but they were already chilled to the bones.

"Oh my gosh!" Emma exclaimed, and jumped back to the carpeted area in the entrance, clutching her jacket against her neck.

Vanesa was startled by the cold, too, but when she looked down at the snow, she saw something on the ground that took her words away. Two pairs of footprints snaked all the way into the whiteness, in the direction of the kids' lodge. Another smaller set of footprints—dog paw prints—went alongside the boot prints. The girls had been lucky. A few more minutes, and the snow would completely cover the clues.

Beck pointed toward the flickering light that seemed to float in the snowstorm. "They must have headed toward the lodge with Rocky. But why?"

"Yes, why would they do that?" asked Emma.

"Who cares why?" Vanesa exclaimed. Hunter would walk across a desert or through a blizzard for a dog, but she didn't have time to explain. A clap of thunder made the ground vibrate.

The three girls shrieked and jumped in place.

"Thunder and snow?" Beck asked, outraged. "How could that happen?"

"I have no idea," said Vanesa. "But I need to get my brother and make sure he's all right." Hunter would be terrified. He hated thunder.

Beck blocked the door. "You're not going anywhere! Look at the weather! Bryce said that in a blizzard, you can lose your way and—"

"I know what he said," Vanesa snapped. "But if we wait any longer, the boys will definitely get lost. The clues will be buried." She stepped onto the soft snow that immediately burned the exposed skin on her ankles. "You do whatever you want. I'm getting my brother."

"And I'm getting Eric!" Emma said, stepping next to Vanesa.

"You can't go out there in slippers!" Beck said.

Vanesa hated that Beck sounded logical. She couldn't argue, and without a word, she stepped back inside. She headed toward the bench where her boots lay surrounded by a puddle of melted snow. Eric's boots were gone! Now there was no doubt that the boys were out there.

"Let's hurry, guys!" Vanesa said. She didn't bother clasping the boot buckles, and she didn't care that she didn't have socks on. Okay, she cared, but only a little. She cared more about her brother than germs.

"Ready," Emma said, grabbing a pair of skis. "Let's go."

"Good idea!" Vanesa grabbed her skis and poles, too, but Beck followed without taking a pair.

Emma shrugged as if to tell Vanesa to let Beck deal with her own consequences.

Without another word, the three girls took off in the direction of the single light burning on the top floor of the kids' lodge.

Chapter Nine
Ain't No Mountain High Enough

Emma clicked her boots onto the skis and used the poles to propel herself toward the kids' lodge, her braids whipping in the wind behind her. Beck trudged on as if the snow didn't bother her. She looked like a real-life version of Elsa, the snow queen. Cold and angry.

Skiing would be faster than trudging through the snow. Vanesa tried to clasp her boot onto the first ski, but her buckle was truly busted after her fall from the lift and the skidding stop. She stomped as hard as she could, but all that happened was that the buckle came off the ski completely. The snow fell into her eyes, and the wind snatched a word from her lips that wasn't really bad, but that she'd never use in front of her parents.

Great. Would she have to pay for the broken skis now? Her allowance didn't cover much more than treats at the movies, and added to the minibar treats that Hunter had devoured, she'd never earn enough to pay her parents back.

"Come on!" Emma called through the wind.

Beck was watching Vanesa struggle with her ski, but she didn't even offer to help. Huffing, Vanesa put all her weight on the broken ski so it wouldn't slide from underneath her foot. She tried to push herself forward with the poles. It didn't work. She didn't have gloves or a hat, and soon her hands were frozen. She switched technique and tried to walk in a shuffle, but the broken ski kept slipping off ahead of her or staying stuck behind.

Vanesa lost her balance and fell hard on her bum. Beck ran ahead, looking the other way as she did so as if trying to hide her smile, but Vanesa saw her. Vanesa was sure she *did* look ridiculous, but why was Beck being so mean? At least the Darlings wouldn't see her like this.

The Darlings! Vanesa needed to get her phone back so they wouldn't think she was ignoring the group.

This was all Beck's fault.

Although, the annoying little voice in her head told Vanesa that if *she* hadn't left Hunter alone, none of this would've happened.

"I know! I know! Okay?" she mumbled out loud.

Ahead, Emma and Beck turned to look at her, but they couldn't have possibly heard her, could they?

Vanesa refocused on her skis. Only one ski had clicked into her boot right. Then she remembered the only lesson Bryce had taught them today: You can slide on one foot.

But she couldn't push herself with the poles while carrying her broken ski. She wanted to ask for help, but she also didn't want to ask Beck for anything. She didn't even want to give her the chance to say no.

She dropped the broken ski and left it behind. She'd be back for it later.

"Ay, Vane, Vane," she said to herself aloud and cringed because she sounded *just* like Mami. "Why do you get yourself into so many problems?"

She didn't know the answer. She'd planned to stay out of trouble, but here she was, heading into a whiteout without knowing for sure her brother was in the kids' lodge. What if he was safe and sound eating marshmallows in the main building? What if Papi had found him?

Why did she keep ruining every family vacation because of her rash decisions?

That day of her twelfth birthday party, Vanesa had left Hunter alone in the trampoline place for just a minute. She realized Amber was in the other room with all the food, and she hadn't reminded her parents that Amber was highly allergic to gluten. Like deadly allergic. She had to go tell them. Hunter, who had no sense of time, felt that the one minute was an eternity and went looking for Vanesa. He ended up walking into a high-stakes game of kickball.

The ball hit Hunter right in the face with the force of a cannonball. Vanesa, who couldn't find the party room in the chaos of a Saturday afternoon, found her brother wandering around the trampoline place, crying his eyes out. His face was covered in blood.

Even now, instead of the pine and snow, it was the sharp scent of her brother's blood that pierced her nose. She wasn't sure if the wind or the guilt was making her cheeks burn.

When she took her brother to her parents in the party room that day, she found out Amber had eaten a cookie that had been labeled gluten-free by mistake. She had the worst allergic reaction of her life.

Amber kicked Vanesa out of the Sunshine Darlings. Vanesa couldn't believe it, since *she'd* been the one to name their group at the beginning of the year. But what Amber said, Peyton and Rory agreed with. She was out.

Vanesa had tried her best to show that she was committed to their friendship, but Amber still hadn't forgiven Vanesa.

After many messages and conversations, weeks and weeks after the *incident*, Vanesa was finally on probation. Amber would make a decision about Vanesa's status after spring break.

Worst of all, Vanesa couldn't forgive herself. She'd chosen her friend over her own brother, and everything had been a disaster, anyway. She should've watched out for both of them.

She'd promised never to put Hunter in this kind of situation again, and she'd broken that promise. She'd promised

Amber she'd do anything for the group, and she couldn't even keep up the message streak.

She had to save Hunter, and she had to get her phone back.

That thought kept Vanesa sliding on one foot through the snow toward the kids' lodge even when her arms throbbed with the effort. She didn't remember the kids' lodge being so far from the main lodge, but when she looked over her shoulder, she couldn't even see the door she and the other two girls had walked through. She hoped they'd be able to walk back to the main lodge. She turned back, put her head down, and kept sliding until she bumped into Emma full speed.

"I'm sorry!" Vanesa said, shivering. Her boots were insulated, but her feet were numb from the cold. Also, she had a stitch stabbing her side. She'd been breathing through her mouth. Although it was impossible to tell the terrain in the storm, she was pretty sure they had been going uphill.

Emma yelled something again, and when she realized that Vanesa couldn't hear her, she pointed ahead of them.

At first, Vanesa couldn't see a thing, but then the kids' lodge emerged briefly from the white fog and swirl of snow.

Vanesa almost laughed with relief. Was this how the sailors in adventure books felt when they finally caught a glimpse of dry land?

Dry land! Vanesa couldn't wait to arrive, take off her boots, and cozy up by a fire. If only she'd brought her bunny slippers in her pocket!

But no.

She had no intention of staying at the kids' lodge. After she made sure Hunter was okay, the two of them were heading straight back and Hunter would explain to their parents that it hadn't been her fault that he'd gotten lost.

Emma reached the door first. It was locked. She knocked. The wind howled in Vanesa's ears. Cold all the way to her bones, Vanesa knocked, too. This time, frantic barking boomed from the other side.

"Let me try," Beck said, shoving Vanesa aside.

"Don't touch me, you—"

But Beck didn't pay attention to her. She knocked on the door and yelled, "Guys! Open up. You don't want to be in there by yourselves!"

Beck's words, or worse, the way she said them, made the little hairs on Vanesa's neck stand up like pine needles. She pushed Beck out of the way and yelled, "The blizzard is getting worse! We need to go back to the main lodge."

Beck tried to push her back, but the door opened slowly, like the person behind it was peeking out reluctantly— or like the door had swung open on its own. Vanesa started to shrink away, but then she stopped herself. She wasn't a scaredy-cat.

She armed herself with courage. Before she could take a breath to call her brother again, a mountain of hair, slobber, and wagging tail jumped on her and knocked her off her feet. For a second, she was actually in the air.

The abominable snowman! She should've listened to Beck. They should've headed back to the main lodge. How was she ever going to explain this to Mami?

Vanesa landed on her back with a thud. Thankfully, the soft snow cushioned her fall, and she didn't hit her head on the ground. She didn't have a helmet on. What had she been thinking?

Before she could scramble to her feet, a wet doggish tongue was kissing her. Yuck!

This was worse than a yeti. It was Rocky the dog!

Whiskers poked her cheeks. "Help me," Vanesa called. "Help!" She couldn't untangle from Rocky's slobbery attack. But Beck ignored her. She stood to the side, rubbing her face. A ski pole lay at her feet.

This was it. Vanesa crossed Beck out of her heart and mind; she didn't want anything to do with the girl even if she did turn out to be a celebrity.

"Easy, boy," a little voice said.

With a strength she didn't know she possessed, Vanesa pushed Rocky aside and jumped to her feet. "Hunter!" she exclaimed.

Chapter Ten
The Kids' Kingdom

Vanesa scooped her brother up in a hug so tight that he groaned. "I can't breathe."

Laughing, Vanesa put him down.

"Let them in!" another voice called from inside the cabin.

"Eric!" cried out Emma. After unclicking her boots from the skis like a pro, she jumped into the cabin and her brother's arms.

Vanesa, unable to help herself, kissed the top of her own brother's head. His hair was wet and smelled of their shampoo from back home: a combination of lavender and lemon.

"What in the world are you doing here?" she asked, and then her eyes bore down on Eric. "Didn't you hear what Bryce said? That we shouldn't go out on our own?"

Eric rolled his eyes. "Chill, girl."

"Eric," Emma said in a warning voice.

He turned around quickly to face his sister and exclaimed, "Stop talking to me like you're my mom! And close the door, guys! You're going to freeze!"

Vanesa had to admit he was right—the wind was sharp and painful. Vanesa looked over her shoulder toward the main lodge. She couldn't see a single light. If she didn't know any better, she would have thought that there was no building there. It was as if the snow had swallowed Pinecloud.

Now, *this* was a whiteout.

When she was younger, Vanesa had read *Sarah, Plain and Tall*. When she reached the part where Papa tied a rope from the barn to the cabin so no one would get lost when they went out to milk the cows, she had a hard time imagining why they'd do such a thing. Now she understood. Would the resort people have a similar system? A series of ropes back to the main lodge?

Bryce would know, like he'd known it was too dangerous to venture out.

The wind was so strong they had a hard time closing the door behind them. Then Vanesa turned around and looked at the kids' lodge. It was like a dream, with overstuffed chairs, a giant TV, and even a popcorn machine! If she'd had her phone, Vanesa would actually love spending the rest of the day here, away from her parents' all-seeing eyes. But her parents would worry about her and Hunter. And she *needed* her phone. She had to get back.

Rocky led the way to the sofas, heaving his big body onto the cushions first.

The lodge was decorated like an exact replica of the main lodge, except that everything was smaller here. The fireplaces, the sofas, even the pictures of Annabeth Grant on the wall. Beck had said that this was the original cabin. Vanesa was curious to know more about this place. But right now, she was more concerned with being stuck. The howling wind was muffled by the door, but Vanesa still heard it roaring inside her head. The girls had arrived right before the storm worsened. And why had Beck said the boys didn't want to be here on their own? She'd been reading that book. Did she know something she wasn't telling them?

At least Hunter was okay. His little hands were so warm in Vanesa's numb ones. He was safe. But what was he doing here?

Vanesa turned on Eric again and asked, "What were you thinking? Why did you bring him here?"

Her outburst rang inside the cabin louder than the wind outside. Eric raised a finger at her. "First of all, he's the one that brought me here—"

"Are you for real?" Vanesa said, slapping her thigh for emphasis like Mami did when they argued. "Are you really going to blame a little kid? He's only seven!"

Beck stood to the side, doing the chameleon thing where you pretended to blend in with the surroundings. Vanesa had tried the technique at school, but it had never worked.

"Let him explain," Emma said, taking a step toward Eric. Of course. He was her brother. But Vanesa had had enough.

"Well?" she demanded of Eric. "Why are you guys here?"

"Vane!" Hunter's little voice called her. He pulled on her arm. When she looked down, his eyes were anxious and teary as if he'd been trying to get her attention for a while now.

She lowered her head to hear. He whispered in her ear. His breath tickled her, but she couldn't understand the words.

"You need to speak up, Huntercito," she said, using Mami's nickname for him.

Hunter's huge eyes scanned the room. He wiped his runny nose with the back of his hand and said, "It's totally my fault, not Eric's. Rocky took me out here. I'm fine."

As if he knew Hunter was talking about him, Rocky tilted his head to the side and then barked. The loud sound reverberated inside the close quarters of the kids' lodge. Emma, Eric, and Beck laughed, but Vanesa hadn't recovered from the fright. The dog needed to learn to stay quiet when he wasn't part of the conversation.

Rocky jumped off the sofa and moved toward Vanesa. She stepped back, but the wall cut off her escape. The dog lay at her feet and lowered his ears. He whined and rolled to the side.

"He wants you to rub his tummy," Hunter said, nudging Vanesa toward the dog. He sniffled.

Vanesa shook her head. "No! I'm not touching him!"

Immediately, four pairs of eyes looked at her with horror, but Vanesa was more worried about her brother's runny nose.

Once Hunter started sniffling, the sneezing and low fever followed. It was only a matter of time before his cough started. And if he didn't take his asthma medicine soon, the cough could worsen in a matter of minutes. But the others wouldn't understand.

Hunter, oblivious to the danger he was in, was already on the ground wrestling with Rocky. Rocky growled playfully and rolled on his back from side to side. A trail of slobber stretched from his smiling face to the wooden floors.

"Gross!" said Vanesa. "Hunter, how is it Rocky's fault that you're here?"

But Hunter didn't seem to hear her. Beck was kneeling next to Rocky and Hunter while Vanesa plopped on one of the fluffy couches that faced the fireplace. A cold draft blew from it, and Vanesa shivered. Now that she knew Hunter was okay, she took off her boots and massaged her feet— they started to hurt even more now that she was warming up. She clenched her teeth to stop the tears that burned in her eyes. She didn't want the others to think she was crying about being stranded here in the cabin. Because she wasn't. She'd never cry about something she could actually solve.

Frustrated, she changed tactics. "Eric," she said, "sorry that I yelled at you. I was just so scared for my brother."

"Yeah," Emma added. "We were scared for you, Eric. *How* did you end up here?"

Eric plopped on the couch opposite Vanesa, and Emma sat down next to him. Following Vanesa's example, she took off her boots, too.

"First of all," Eric said, with his index finger up again. "I was on my way to get s'mores."

"S'more of what?" Beck asked, speaking up for the first time.

Vanesa understood the reference to one of her family's favorite movies, but Eric and Emma obviously didn't because their faces were like human question marks. Vanesa didn't make even the slightest sign that she'd understood.

Eric rolled his eyes dramatically and said, "As I was saying, I was on my way to get s'mores in the main lodge when out of the blue comes little Hunter telling me that he needed help. I ran to the hallway downstairs, and there's the dog."

"The dog?" Vanesa asked, and Rocky whined as though he were saying *Who, me?* Seriously. The dog needed better manners.

"And Rocky led us out into the snow—we trusted him," Eric said.

Hunter was still on the ground, playing with Rocky and Beck. Vanesa tried to catch what they were saying, but they stopped talking as if they didn't want Vanesa to hear. Her heart fell. It always happened this way. Hunter charmed everyone until there was no one left to be her friend. Except for Amber. She was the only friend Hunter hadn't stolen.

She and Vanesa had become sort-of friends at the end of sixth grade, when Amber was taking a break from Peyton and Rory. Funny that she was now the one out of the group, and all because of a cookie! Vanesa twirled the bracelet with her fingers. She hated that it was brown.

Emma was hammering Eric with questions.

He listened in silence, brushing his hand over his head like he was used to having long hair and had a hard time breaking the habit.

"You went out in this weather, Eric? Are you a baby or what? You're turning twelve years old tomorrow."

"Tonight," he said.

Emma replied, "Whatever."

It seemed like the twins had had this interaction a million times, with Emma always the one coming out on top.

Eric blushed again, and his eyes hardened. "I know that it's my twelfth birthday tonight, Emma. I'm not a baby. It wasn't really snowing this hard when we followed Bryce out, you know?"

Vanesa's ears perked. "Wait, Bryce came with you? Why would he go out into the snow like that?"

"Rocky was following him here. We kept calling to him, but he had earmuffs on."

"Well, then where is he?" Vanesa exclaimed.

Thunder made the windows rattle again, swallowing her words. It could have been Vanesa's imagination, or it could've been the wind, but she thought she heard a voice calling out for help. When she stayed still so she could hear better, the only thing she heard was her thudding heart in her ears.

Chapter Eleven
The Ham

Just as the windows stopped shaking from the thunder, Hunter sneezed. Vanesa said, "Salud," automatically, but then she looked at her brother with dread. She hoped that word had any kind of power at all to keep him with health, at least long enough to get back to the main lodge. She thought with regret of his inhaler, sitting there on the dresser when she'd left. Why hadn't she taken it with her, just in case?

Seeing Vanesa's expression, Emma asked, "What's wrong?"

"Shh," Vanesa said, putting a finger on her mouth and willing her ears to sharpen up and hear better. "Do you hear that?"

Immediately, all the kids went quiet, looking at Vanesa for an explanation. Even Beck, who now stood by the window looking at how fast the snow was piling up, seemed alert, like she didn't want to miss any of Vanesa's words.

"I think I hear something," she said.

Eric had flopped onto the floor with Rocky and Hunter, who looked like he was in heaven—like he had his own dog *and* an older brother. *Poor Hunter*, Vanesa thought. He was stuck with her. And even though she saw how much he loved Rocky, she couldn't help being afraid of dogs ever since the chasing incident. Every time she saw one, her anxiety rose and her hands and feet prickled. When she remembered that dogs could smell fear, her heart went berserk.

Even if she knew this dog was trained to save lives, her body had a memory of its own and broke into shivers every time she made eye contact with Rocky. No, she wouldn't pretend she liked the dog, not even if it hurt Hunter's feelings.

And now this eerie sound spooked her. Did fear have different smells? Rocky didn't seem to smell a thing.

Eric rested on his elbow and said, "Rocky's wagging that giant tail like a fool. If something was wrong, he wouldn't look so happy." He looked at Emma with a pointed expression. "And speaking of happy, I thought Bryce would burst into tears of joy when he realized it was Hunter and I walking through the door."

"If something *were* wrong," Emma corrected. "Hunter and *me*. Your grammar is atrocious, Eric."

Her words felt surprisingly sharp. Eric looked like Emma had slapped him.

In Eric's place, Vanesa would have replied with even crueler words. The fight would have snowballed and avalanched and trapped her until she didn't know how to get out of the mess.

Eric, on the other hand, brushed his shoulder off and stood up. Vanesa was impressed by how tall he seemed all of a sudden. Taller than he actually was.

Eric didn't even look at his sister. Instead, he looked at Vanesa and said, "Let's go find Bryce. He went upstairs. He can tell you what happened. Last I saw him, he told us to stay put, but I want to go back to my parents."

He said *my parents* with more ice in his voice than what frosted the windows. Hunter was so immersed in petting Rocky that he was oblivious to the fight. Emma sat next to Beck, who stared at the window with fear. There was nothing to see, other than the reflection of what was happening in the room. Beck seemed to be far away in her own thoughts. Why was she so scared? And if there really was something to be scared of, why didn't she tell everyone? Her attitude was starting to scare Vanesa, too.

Vanesa followed Eric upstairs, turning every light on as she went. "Is Hunter telling the truth?" she asked. "Was Rocky with him the whole time?"

Eric shrugged. "Rocky wouldn't leave his side. He seemed like he didn't want Bryce to go out alone. Then when he saw the tennis balls in the container by the entrance, I guess he got distracted."

Vanesa remembered seeing a giant bucket with neon-green tennis balls by the front door.

"Bryce!" Eric called, walking ahead of Vanesa.

The staircase was narrow and its ceiling so low, Vanesa could reach it if she stood on her tiptoes. The eyes of the people in the old-fashioned paintings followed her as she walked past.

She heard a rustling sound ahead and flinched. "What's that?" she whispered.

A voice spoke, but it sounded like the person was speaking from the end of a tunnel. "Is that you, kids?"

It was Bryce. Vanesa breathed easier. He really was here. He wasn't exactly a grown-up, but at least she didn't have to be the one in charge. Beck was acting weird. Emma and Eric fought nonstop. That left her in charge of making decisions, and she didn't want to be in charge. What if she messed up? Now that Bryce was here, he could take control of the situation.

"Bryce," she said, following Eric onto a wide landing: a loft that looked like a play area or library. There were bookcases covering the walls and a chess set on a coffee table. The same smell of wood polish from the main lodge made Vanesa's nose itch.

Bryce looked up. He'd had his face buried in a cardboard box. When he saw her, he didn't look happy.

"What in the world are you doing here?" he asked. "Didn't you see how dangerous it was outside? Didn't you hear the thunder?"

Seeing a scolding coming, Eric turned right around. "I'm going back to the couches!" he said.

Vanesa started to answer Bryce, but more thunder drowned her words.

"How can there be thunder in a snowstorm? That's impossible," she said when it stopped. The sound of Hunter and Beck laughing downstairs sparked a bout of frustration in her. How could her brother be so happy when they were in this situation? Wasn't Hunter terrified of thunder? What had Beck said that was so funny?

"Actually," Bryce said, "it sounds like it's a thundersnow storm. I noticed the greenish tinge in the clouds when we were waiting for you and Emma to finally slide down from the blue slope. You kids were too distracted, but I noticed."

"And you didn't tell us?" Vanesa asked, outraged.

Bryce raised his eyebrows and said, "I did tell you. You and your friends weren't paying attention. I said it was too dangerous to go out."

He *had* said that. "Well, then, why did you come out here?" Vanesa asked. "Hunter and Eric said they just followed you!"

Bryce looked suddenly sheepish. "I had to put all the equipment away, and I figured I could make it out here and back in time. Rocky didn't seem like he wanted me to go, but I ignored him . . . and then I guess he tried to get me help."

"And Rocky thought my little brother could help?"

Bryce waved his hand, brushing off her question. "Hunter and Eric followed Rocky, who followed me. It's exactly what Rocky has been trained to do, *but*," he said, wagging his index finger, "they shouldn't have come out into the snow."

And now all of them were here. At least Hunter was safe—for now. "I have to tell my parents that Hunter is okay," Vanesa said. "Did you call the main lodge to tell anyone he's safe?"

"Yes, I called the front desk as soon as he and Eric showed up. I heard that your parents were looking for him."

"I was looking for him, too," Vanesa said.

"I didn't know that. I told Luís that I'd bring them back to the main lodge, but now I'm worried about the whiteout. And more of you followed them here!"

Vanesa clasped a hand over her mouth. What a mess!

Rocky had tried to help Bryce, and Hunter and Eric had followed Rocky—and then Vanesa and the girls had followed *them*. And now they were all stuck, without a way to get back.

"So now my parents don't know he's still here?" she asked.

Bryce smirked. "Of course they do! I called the lodge again as soon as I decided we couldn't head out yet. They don't know you're here, though."

Vanesa sighed. She should've stayed behind!

"I need to call my parents," she said.

Bryce passed her an old-fashioned phone. It had a curly cord and big buttons. It was like the one Abuela Bea had in her house in Buenos Aires. "Here," he said. "Dial the number on the sticker on the back of the receiver and then ask Luís to connect you to your parents."

She did. The phone rang a few times and then went to voice mail. Her heart sank. "No answer," she said.

Bryce stopped rummaging in his bag and said, "Keep trying."

Vanesa dialed the number again, and this time, Luís answered before the first ring. "Pinecloud Lodge, how may I help you?"

"Luís," she said. Her voice sounded so small in the

receiver. "It's Vanesa Campos. Can you transfer me to my parents? Please?"

"Nossa Senhora!" Luís exclaimed. He muttered something else in Portuguese that Vanesa didn't catch. He cleared his throat, and back in his super professional voice, he said, "Miss Campos, your parents have been worried sick. Tell me please, are the other two girls with you? Emma Mae Richardson and Rebecca Hansen?"

The urgency in his voice made her nervous. "Y-y-yes," she said. "We're in the kids' lodge, safe and sound."

"Thank goodness! We saw that two pairs of skis were gone, and we thought you girls had headed to the slopes!"

Vanesa rolled her eyes, grateful Luís couldn't see her. She was rash, but she wasn't dumb. How could anyone think she'd headed to the slopes in a whiteout? But then, who could've imagined she and the other girls would head out to the kids' lodge when they couldn't see where they were going? What if they'd fallen over a cliff? She shivered while Luís went on and on about how happy he was that the girls were okay.

"I'll transfer you to your parents. Now, stay there with Bryce and the other kids. Have fun until the storm dies down, and then we'll get you back here."

"But I—" Vanesa didn't want to *stay here*. Not with the slobbering dog, the snobbish Beck, and the fighting twins.

"Hello." Mami's voice echoed in the phone. "Vanesa, is that you?"

"Yes, Mami, it's me. I'm okay."

"Thank goodness," Mami said. "I was worried you'd gone back out skiing, but I knew not even you could be so reckless. Stay there with that boy Bryce. The Grant brothers say he's very responsible. And take care of your bro—" The connection flickered.

"Mami," Vanesa said, "I don't want to stay here. Can Papi come get me?"

Nobody answered. Mami wasn't on the other end of the line anymore.

Vanesa dialed the number again, but there was no sound. Just in case, she dialed her mom's cell number (the only one she knew by heart), but there was only silence.

"The phone died," Vanesa said, resigned.

Bryce took his cell phone out of his pocket, and Vanesa's heart did a flip of excitement that died as soon as Bryce closed his eyes, disappointed. "No cell signal, no internet . . . Uncle Zachariah should've listened to me! I told him satellite internet wouldn't work here."

"But aren't the phones separate?" Vanesa asked.

Bryce shook his head. "This building is so old that the whole wiring had to be newly placed when they remodeled it. Zachariah, wanting to be modern and all, had a satellite internet antenna placed on the roof and connected the phone to it. But now the internet is out, and so is the phone. The antenna must be covered with snow."

"Well then," Vanesa said. "Can you get up there and clean it?"

Bryce stared at her wordlessly.

The ticktock of an old grandfather clock worsened the charged silence.

Vanesa tried a different tactic. "Don't you have a walkie-talkie?" she asked, not wanting to give up.

Bryce's face went red like a tomato. "I can't find it. I thought I dropped it in one of these boxes by accident."

"And what were you looking for in the boxes?"

Bryce kept rummaging, more frustrated by the minute. "A ham radio."

Vanesa had never heard of a ham radio before. A radio made of ham? "How is that going to help us?"

Bryce, guessing her confusion, laughed, and she felt like he was making fun of her.

"A ham radio, you know? Named after radio geniuses Hertz, Armstrong, and Marconi?"

He stared at her for a few seconds, but she had no idea what he was talking about.

"What are they teaching in schools these days?" Bryce looked sad, which made Vanesa feel worse than when he had laughed. "It's an old-fashioned radio. It's independent, you see? I even have a license."

An old-fashioned radio that didn't depend on the internet to work? And Bryce even had a license? "Sweet!" Vanesa exclaimed.

Obviously encouraged by Vanesa's reaction, Bryce continued, "I had a hunch that communications would go down someday, but Zachariah, Uncle Zachariah, that is, told me not to worry. And now that cells and the internet are down, we could do well with an old-fashioned radio."

"Where is it?" Vanesa asked, looking inside a box that contained brochures.

Bryce shrugged. "Good question! Zachariah thinks cleaning up means putting things in boxes. Who knows where he left it!" Bryce continued searching the room, but unless the radio was hidden among the books on the shelves, Vanesa didn't hold her breath that it would be here. Still, she helped him look, even though he hadn't asked her to.

"If I had the walkie, at least! I swear I put it inside my backpack," Bryce muttered.

"Where's your backpack?" asked Vanesa.

"I have no idea, Miss Vanesa, or believe me, I'd have already found it. If possible, I don't want to be here in the nighttime, and look," he said, pointing at the window. They could hardly see the snowflakes falling. "It's already almost dark."

A chill snaked around Vanesa's ankles as though the frigid wind had found a way inside. But she didn't even see a vent where the air could blow in. Again, the little hairs on her neck prickled.

"Why don't you want to be here at night?" she asked, dreading his answer.

Bryce looked over his shoulder at Vanesa, his eyes wide with fear. This did nothing to make her feel better. "I don't really want to say, but . . . it's my great-great-great-aunt Annabeth," he whispered.

"Annabeth Grant?" Vanesa asked, stepping closer to Bryce in spite of herself. "She's your great-great-great aunt? Didn't she live in the 1800s? Hasn't she been dead for ages?"

Bryce shook his head and placed a finger over his lips. "Shhhh! Don't speak so loudly! Everyone knows her ghost still haunts this place, the place she loved the most in the world!"

Vanesa couldn't have heard right. Her *ghost*?

Hunter, Beck, Eric, and Emma laughed at something downstairs. But upstairs, Rocky whined. Vanesa jumped—she hadn't heard the dog come up. Rocky put his head down and covered his ears with his paws.

Bryce walked up to Vanesa and whispered, "Her ghost lives in the attic."

As soon as the words were out of his mouth, the lights flickered off.

Chapter Twelve
The Hunt for Jolly Ranchers

Vanesa screamed.

Being stranded in a cabin with her brother, a dog, kids who couldn't stop fighting, and an incompetent ski instructor was already a worst-case scenario. With a ghost and a power outage added to the equation, Vanesa knew enough math to calculate that the probability for disaster was high.

Maybe with a phone she could've made the best out of this situation. She could have taken a video of Bryce freaking out—he was now screaming, too—and the rest of the kids panicking downstairs. That kind of thing would go viral in a matter of minutes. But now, without a phone, the chance of becoming a celebrity for a funny video was out the window. Never mind calling her parents back.

"Stay here for a second," Bryce said when he recovered. "I'm going to make sure the other babies are okay."

"Babies?" Vanesa repeated in the darkness of the playroom. Had she missed another whole group of kids, of babies? Then realization fell on her. "Wait, *what*?" Did that make *her* a baby, too? She fumed.

Bryce didn't reply. At the sound of his footsteps heading toward the stairs, Vanesa exclaimed, "I don't want to stay on this floor so close to the attic!" She tried to follow him, but she could hardly see a couple of steps ahead. The sunlight was quickly disappearing as the storm picked up.

Bryce said anxiously, "But we need to find the radio or the walkie-talkie. They have to be up here. Someone has to search while there's a little bit of light left. Rocky will stay here to protect you."

Vanesa flinched. She didn't want to be anywhere close to Rocky—or the ghost in the attic. But Bryce was right about finding a way to communicate with the lodge. Even though she didn't like the dog, she felt a little better in his presence.

"I promise I'll be back as soon as possible," Bryce said, and left.

Vanesa heard footsteps again as he slowly went down the stairs. She pressed her forehead against the cold window and felt the strength of the wind. What if it broke the glass? The thought made her heart gallop, so she stepped back a little and looked outside.

There was a glow, as if the fog and the snow were playing tag with a light that shone through the swirling flakes. Vanesa tried to focus her eyes and saw the outline of the main lodge. Lights were on in the windows there.

They still had electricity!

Mami and Papi must think she and Hunter were having the time of their lives. They'd have no idea the power had gone out in the kids' lodge. If only she could let them know!

The wind seemed to change direction because suddenly, she caught a glimpse of the signpost that led to the slopes and its glowing light on top. It stood between the lodges like a lighthouse. On the ground, there was a shadow. It could either be an animal, crouching against the pole to protect itself from the elements, or forgotten ski equipment . . . or maybe it was Bryce's backpack!

Running footsteps approached behind her. Vanesa turned to see Bryce, enveloped in a circle of yellow light. He held Hunter by the hand. Hunter had tears streaming down his cheeks. Rocky rushed to his side and started licking his face.

Vanesa pushed Rocky out of the way and knelt in front of Hunter. Rocky's hot breath tickled her neck, but the dog seemed so worried about Hunter that Vanesa didn't have the heart to shoo him away.

"Let's go back with Mami and Papi!" Hunter begged. "We can't watch ninjas or play *DragonVille* here. There's no electricity."

Bryce carefully placed the emergency candle, the kind that lasts more than a hundred hours, on a table. Then he started putting away the boxes. "You didn't find it?" he asked Vanesa.

"What? The radio?" Vanesa said. "I don't even know what a ham radio looks like!"

Bryce sighed, frustrated. Before she wasted more energy on Bryce, Vanesa's attention went back to her brother.

"We'll be okay, Huntercito," she said. "We're together. And soon we'll be with Mami and Papi, okay?"

He nodded. His tears spilled onto Vanesa's sweatshirt when he hugged her tightly, but she didn't complain. He was so little. When she lowered her head, she was shocked at how hot his skin felt.

"Oh no!" Vanesa said. "Hunter, I think you have a fever!"

Hunter's only reply was a cough. It was the kind of dry cough that made him sound like a dog. Then he burst into more tears.

"I left my inhaler in the room," he said between hiccups. "Did you bring it?"

She shook her head, upset with herself, and her brother cried harder.

Papi had once explained to Vanesa that fear of what could happen during an asthma attack (the tightness in his chest, a trip to the hospital where he'd be endlessly poked) made Hunter panic. And then his symptoms would get worse. She needed to calm him down.

Vanesa tried to hold him, but he was too scared and didn't want her to. He shoved her away.

Bryce muttered under his breath but was next to Hunter in two quick strides. Vanesa stood up and moved aside for him to check on her brother. Her knees throbbed.

"Hey, bud. Let me see if you have a fever really," Bryce said softly.

Hunter nodded and stood still while Bryce placed a hand on Hunter's forehead. A pang stabbed at Vanesa's heart. Hunter would never forgive her for being the worst sister in the world. He'd be traumatized forever, and all because of her.

Why hadn't she grabbed the inhaler?

She'd only thought of herself. Of getting the bed and her phone to take *fake* pictures to make her *friends* jealous.

Bryce smiled at Hunter and said, "It's just that you must have a fast metabolism, and fast engines run hot. I'm sure it's nothing else. Now, let's go back down and have some snacks with the other kids. We can have an inside campout. What do you think?"

His upbeat suggestion calmed Hunter down. But when Bryce glanced up at Vanesa, his face was an open book. And Vanesa, being the Reader of the Year, could read the fear in Bryce's expression.

Bryce knew that Hunter wasn't doing too well, but he didn't want to scare him.

Vanesa felt worry bubbling inside her as she and Hunter followed Bryce downstairs, guided by the faint glow of the candle he held ahead of them.

Five more hundred-hour candles were scattered around the room, and for a moment, Vanesa thought the area looked super cozy. Eric was on one of the couches with a blanket wrapped around him, looking sleepy. Beck and Emma sat at a table. UNO cards were scattered in front of them, but they'd been talking, not playing. The old book with the history of Annabeth Grant lay open next to Beck. *Was there another copy in the cabin?* Vanesa wondered. She hadn't noticed Beck bringing a book on their trek from the main lodge.

By the alarm on their faces, Vanesa guessed they'd been discussing the resident ghost, and once again, she felt the chill in the air snake down her spine. She shivered.

The other two girls had mugs of hot chocolate and a bowl of popcorn between them, but it all looked untouched.

Eric hopped up from the couch and grabbed a handful of popcorn. He chewed loudly and asked, "How long have we been here? It looks like midnight." He pointed out the window. The snow had accumulated a couple of feet high. If this continued, they'd be trapped under tons of snow.

They all seemed to sense the urgency, so when Bryce started talking, no one interrupted him.

"My friends, we're safe here in this cabin," he declared. "We can try to weather the night. In the morning, Zachariah and Josiah will drive the truck to dig us out."

"But there's no electricity, no phones, and no internet! We're kids: We can't live without our electronic devices!" Eric complained.

Vanesa silently agreed with him. If she lost her texting streak, she could never go back to school.

"It's already getting colder!" Vanesa pointed out, trying not to think about the ghost.

"We can light a fire," Bryce said.

"Do you even know how?" Emma asked. She'd been too quiet until now.

"Of course I know how!" But Vanesa could hear the hesitation in Bryce's voice. She was sure the others heard it, too. "In any case," Bryce said, "we can get tents and other supplies from the storage. If we're all inside a tent, we can keep warm."

"We need to go back for our birthday," Emma said, glancing at Eric, her voice trembling.

"There's no reason to panic," repeated Bryce, but this time, he didn't sound so convinced.

Beck spoke next. "Bryce, what are the chances of us getting back to the main lodge tonight?"

"Zero," Bryce said. He gave Beck a pointed look and motioned toward Hunter, who crouched on the floor next to Rocky. "Little man needs his medicine, but if we keep him comfortable and calm, we could wait until the morning."

Beck crossed her arms pointedly. After a few seconds, she said, "Not that I love the idea, but I've lived through a few snowmageddons, and actually Bryce is right. It's better if we stay put."

Just when Vanesa was going to argue, more thunder and the tapping of branches against the windows drowned her words. Everyone looked *shook*, except for Hunter, who was still clueless about the ghost of Annabeth Grant. Vanesa wanted to keep it that way. If he got more scared, the cough would worsen. Hunter couldn't risk an asthma attack right now.

"I'm going to the storage room to get the tent. I'm pretty sure we have some candy there. Do you like Jolly Ranchers, Hunter?" Bryce asked.

Hunter nodded, but he had another bout of coughing. The kids exchanged looks of alarm.

"I'll be right back," Bryce said. "Wish me luck."

He left, taking one of the never-ending candles, while the wind howled like a pack of wolves.

Vanesa had a sudden thought: In all the suspense movies and books, splitting up was always a bad idea.

"Wait!" Vanesa called after Bryce. "Take someone with you!"

But Bryce was already gone. In the hallway that led to the stairs, deformed shadows danced on the wall. Vanesa looked away quickly because one of them looked like a woman with wild hair, beckoning her with a curled finger.

Chapter Thirteen
Old-Timey Wonder Woman

Vanesa looked around at the group. "Do you want to play UNO?" she asked Hunter. When he said yes, she dealt the cards.

Eric and Emma joined Vanesa and Hunter in the game. Beck sat, stiff-backed, on the couch, looking at pictures on her phone. Vanesa didn't repeat her invitation. If Beck wanted to act all high and mighty, she was welcome to, but she had to think of the greater good. How selfish was she, playing on her phone as if nothing had happened?

"You might want to save some battery, Rebecca," Vanesa said. "The cell signal might come back, and we could call the main lodge with your phone."

Beck pretended Vanesa hadn't spoken and took a selfie. The sound of the camera shutter grated on Vanesa's ears.

Eric and Emma won the first round of UNO. Hunter's face fell, so Vanesa suggested they all play solo for the next round. Hunter lit up again, but Emma glanced at Eric and then sent Vanesa a hesitant look. "Are you sure?" she asked.

Eric stared at her and asked, "What do you mean, Emma? Why do you always have to get in my business? I'm not a baby!"

Emma put her hands up and said, "Whoa, whoa. Chill, bro. I only meant what I asked. 'Are you sure?' Maybe Hunter would be better off playing with Vanesa. I wasn't talking about you!"

But they all knew she had been talking about Eric.

Vanesa and Hunter exchanged a look, and then she glanced away so she wouldn't start laughing. But Hunter couldn't hold his giggles. Eric sulked during the next round as he buried Emma with Draw Four cards.

With each horrible card Eric threw for Emma to pick, a feeling in Vanesa's gut intensified. She couldn't shake it. By the time Rocky padded into the kitchen without Bryce, her ears started ringing. But she brushed it off, thinking that maybe it was the altitude or, worst case, an impending ear infection.

She remembered Abuela Bea's words: *Never ignore your intuition. Trust yourself.*

When Vanesa hadn't followed that advice, she always regretted it. In most cases, a mistake could've been solved quickly if she'd trusted herself more. But usually, she tended to give up everything for lost and make the situation worse. And now, what could this tingling feeling mean?

She was so distracted that she only snapped out of her thoughts when Hunter pulled on her shirt and pointed at Emma and Eric.

The twins were standing at opposite sides of the table, yelling at each other. Vanesa couldn't even understand a word of what they were shouting because Rocky had joined the fight with sharp barks that made her ears feel like they were bleeding. Beck watched with wide eyes from the couch, and Hunter quickly joined her, trying to put as much distance between himself and the fight as possible.

Finally, Vanesa couldn't take it anymore. "Stop!" she yelled at the twins. "You guys are *both* acting like babies!"

Emma and Eric gaped at her.

"Haven't you noticed Bryce hasn't come back?" Vanesa asked. "It's been forever since he went to the storage room to get the tent—"

"And the candy," added Hunter with his little index finger up. He looked so comical that the awkward vibe lightened, even if only a bit.

Yet this bad feeling Vanesa had about Bryce wouldn't go away. "I don't think he would leave us, right?" she asked. "Not without Rocky. I mean, the storm is still raging outside."

No one answered her, but at least no one was fighting.

Quick rapping sounds made Vanesa startle. She wasn't the only one.

"What's that sound?" Hunter asked, looking around.

Eric said, "Maybe it's the ghost . . ."

"Eric!" Emma exclaimed, and she swatted his arm.

Hunter nuzzled against Beck, and Vanesa felt a surge of jealousy that made her see red. But she was angrier at Eric for scaring her brother. "Why would you say that?"

"Bryce *was* scared of the ghost," Eric said, crossing his

arms and stepping away from Emma so she couldn't slap his arm again.

"What ghost?" Hunter asked in a voice that made it clear he wouldn't stop asking until he got an answer.

Vanesa knew that as his older sister she had to make something up. "It's only a story, Hunter."

"But I heard the concierge say her name, too. She's real," Hunter said.

Oh no.

Beck turned to face Hunter and, in a super-sweet voice, said, "A woman lived in this cabin back in the mid-1800s."

Vanesa sighed with frustration, but she wanted to know the story, too. So she held her tongue and walked to the window, listening closely to Beck's words.

"Annabeth Grant is, like, the great-great aunt of Zachariah and Josiah or something like that," Beck said. "She lived in the family homestead on her own when her parents died and the rest of her siblings and cousins moved to Salt Lake City. Back in those days, living alone was a big deal for a woman."

"It still is for some of us!" Emma exclaimed. "I only

mention *I'd like* to have my own room, and some people think it means I hate them!" She glared at Eric.

Eric's jaw tightened, and then he returned Emma's look with equal intensity. "Let's talk about interesting people, not attention seekers."

Emma rolled her eyes, but his focus was back on Beck.

"She worked on the railroad, even though it ruined her reputation," Beck went on. "Her biography says she always followed her gut, and she was super successful, even though she failed a lot, too. She lost a lot of money investing in different businesses, but there are rumors that she was a secret spy for the Pinkerton Detective Agency. That she even had a hand in tracing Sundance Kid and Butch Cassidy to Argentina, then finally trapping them in Bolivia!"

"Hey! My parents are from Argentina!" Hunter exclaimed. "We're Argentine-Americans, my sister and me, see?"

Vanesa noticed how shiny Hunter's eyes were and how fast the words stumbled out of his mouth. He looked so pale under the yellow light of the candles. Vanesa was certain his fever was climbing.

"We're Argentines. Like Leo Messi," Hunter added.

"Leo Messi? The soccer god?" asked Eric, brightening.

Vanesa shook her head. "My dad doesn't let us say the s-word. It's fútbol. And Leo Messi isn't a god; he's only the best ever to play the beautiful game. Like Annabeth isn't a ghost, either. She was just a cool woman."

Beck grabbed the book and looked at the cover for a long time. "This book says she promised she'd never leave this cabin; she built it herself. After her death, every time the owners of the property tried to demolish it, something terrible happened. There were accidents and fires, and the workers had terrible dreams that sent them running away."

"Even if all those rumors were true, they don't make her a *bad* ghost," Vanesa insisted. "Or, um, a ghost at all!" she added hastily.

"Why would she take Bryce then?" Beck asked.

"She didn't take Bryce!" said Vanesa, but the look on everyone's face told her she was the only one who thought that. Even Hunter was nodding, his eyes big.

"I heard Bryce mention Annabeth, too," Emma said. "Maybe she sensed his fear."

The wind howled outside, not showing any signs of letting up. Vanesa wanted to run back to her parents. Had she been all on her own, she'd have left long ago. But she had to think of Hunter. She had to keep him safe. And Bryce had said that the best way to prevent Hunter's cough from worsening was by keeping him warm.

She had to do something instead of being scared of shadows.

She left her corner by the window, took a candle, and set out in the direction she'd last seen Bryce go.

"Where are you going?" Beck asked.

Vanesa ignored her and kept walking, but Beck jumped up from the sofa and grabbed her arm.

If Vanesa's glance could pulverize someone on the spot, Beck would've been a pile of dust. She must have seen she'd crossed a line when she grabbed Vanesa because she stepped back and said, "You can't go alone. I'm the one who knows about Annabeth, and I'm older than you—"

Vanesa put up one hand to stop her. She fluttered her eyes and said, "Even if you were the only person who knew the way, I wouldn't go with you. Even if you were rescuing me from disaster, I wouldn't follow you anywhere, Rebecca. Now get out of my way."

Beck stared at her in awe. Even Vanesa was awed at herself. Never in her life had she done something like this—stood up to someone who was being horrible to her.

The air rang with tension, and Beck went back to the couch and plopped down, speechless.

In a small voice, Hunter asked, "Vane, really, where are you going?"

Vanesa knelt in front of him and said, "I'm going to find Bryce and get supplies." When she stood up, she looked at Emma. "Wanna come with me?" she asked.

Emma smiled and nodded. "Of course. I'm not scared of ghosts."

Eric and Beck seemed to shrink at the bite of her words.

"Be careful, Vane," Hunter whispered. "You're the only sister I have."

He was her only little brother, too, and she'd come back to him no matter what.

Following Vanesa's hunch, the two girls walked into the darkness, retracing Bryce's steps.

Chapter Fourteen
I Have a Bad Feeling About This . . .

The candlelight wasn't enough to illuminate every corner of the staircase leading downstairs. Emma stayed close, her arm hooked through Vanesa's.

"That was pretty epic how you talked back to Beck," Emma said.

Vanesa's neck prickled as if someone's eyes were on her. The feeling of being watched persisted. Maybe Beck had decided to join them. She was so annoying, she'd do something like that. But when Vanesa looked over her shoulder, no one was there.

Still, she felt a presence. It wasn't really an eerie feeling, like when she imagined a ghost. Besides, Bryce was still in the cabin, and Vanesa was determined to find him. What if he was in danger and they were just too scared to rescue him? They couldn't turn back now.

She stopped to listen for where the tapping sounds were coming from. Emma bumped into her, and the candle blew out.

Emma yelped.

Someone grabbed Vanesa's hand and pressed it tightly, too tightly. Vanesa's hand was clammy, and she had a hard time breathing. She remembered a story Papi had read to her when she was little, of two friends holding hands at a sleepover to stop being afraid, only to discover the next morning that when they stretched out their hands from their beds, their fingers didn't even reach each other. So, whose hand had they been holding for hours?

"Emma, is it you holding my hand?" Vanesa had to ask.

Emma chuckled, but there was fear in her voice, too. "Vanesa, you're freaking me out. I'm right next to you. I'll squeeze your hand once and you'll know it's me."

Emma squeezed Vanesa's hand, and Vanesa returned the gesture.

"It's you," the girls said in unison, and Emma exclaimed, "Jinx!"

Vanesa felt a playful pinch on the arm. "I hope the pinch was you, too, or else . . ."

Emma laughed nervously, and they kept going. A faint glow pulsated ahead and made their shadows appear larger, more menacing. There was no sign of the woman-shaped shadow Vanesa had seen before. She rushed ahead to find out where the light was coming from.

"It's the candle Bryce took with him!" she cried, lifting it from a small end table. "He must have left it here!"

She used the light from the new candle to inspect their surroundings. It was a small room lined with bookcases, like a wide hallway between other rooms. The only spaces on the walls not covered with books were covered in animal furs and small portraits of Annabeth Grant. A chill ran down Vanesa's spine, but she couldn't look away from one of the paintings. In it, Annabeth was posing in front of a steam engine. Her smile was wide and inviting. She didn't seem like the kind of person who'd return as a ghost, if anyone really could.

"She looks like she was happy," Emma said, pointing at the painting. "I wonder if her family was happy for her or sad."

There were so many things hidden within Emma's voice. Vanesa didn't want to pry, but she asked, "Do you and Eric always fight so much?"

Emma sighed. "No. Well, yes, we do now. We didn't when we were younger, but since we started seventh grade, things are different. I guess growing up is making us grow apart, and he doesn't like it. But I don't think wanting my own room for privacy is a big deal, do you?"

"Not at all!" Vanesa said. Her room was tiny, but better tiny than shared. She was grateful to have her own space. As it was, Hunter was always coming into her room, asking her to let him play with her phone or making a mess when she wanted her things just so. But the more she pushed Hunter away, the more he clung to her. Maybe it was the same with Eric and Emma.

She was about to ask when the tapping sound started again.

"It sounds a little like Morse code, don't you think?" Emma asked.

Even if she had no idea what Morse code sounded like, Vanesa could hear they were getting closer to the source because the sounds were growing louder. It did actually sound like someone was tapping on purpose. There were irregular pauses that didn't seem natural.

"You're right. That sound can't be a coincidence," Vanesa whispered.

Emma said, "That can't be a branch tapping on the roof, now, can it?"

Vanesa held her breath to hear better. The tapping was methodical, intentional. "Maybe . . . ," she said. "But we need to make sure. What if Bryce is trapped? Maybe we should split up to look for him?"

"In the movies, splitting up and going to look for the sound is never a good idea," Emma said, echoing Vanesa's thoughts from earlier exactly.

Emma held on to Vanesa's hand even tighter than before. In spite of what Vanesa thought, it was clear that Emma had no intention of dividing forces.

Upstairs, there was absolute silence. What were the boys and Beck up to? Vanesa hoped Beck wasn't scaring Hunter with more stories about Annabeth Grant. She also hoped Hunter's fever hadn't gone up. She had to get back upstairs quickly.

"Let's go," Vanesa said, and led Emma ahead through a hallway. After a few feet, she stopped. Was that someone singing? Or was it the voice of a person talking to themselves? It sounded too high-pitched, but it also had a deep rumbling. Maybe she was imagining things. She felt a little shiver of anticipation, like when she'd ridden her first roller coaster at Disneyland, click-click-clicking up the tracks toward a drop. She was scared, but she also couldn't wait to solve the mystery.

The air temperature dropped, and she guessed they'd reached the storage area. There was a soft glow from an emergency exit sign that looked super out of place in this cabin from the days of the pioneers. But it helped them see a little better.

"How is that working?" Emma asked, pointing at the sign.

Vanesa looked up. There were no electrical cords connecting it to an outlet. "Batteries?"

Vanesa and Emma kept walking until they reached a heavy metal door with an electronic keypad. Like the sign, it looked out of place in the old-fashioned cabin, obviously something added recently. She tried to open it, but not even the door handle gave way when she put all her weight on it.

She placed her ear on the small gap between the door and the doorjamb. She couldn't hear anything.

Vanesa turned around to look for another possible cause of the sound, when again she heard the voice singing. She was positive that it was a theme song for the TV show Mami and Papi watched at night on the weekends, one for grown-ups with dragons and zombies. The hairs on the back of Vanesa's neck stood up like pins, and she broke out in a cold sweat. Even her hands were sweaty. Vanesa wondered why her brain stored all her scary memories to terrify her even more in the worst moments. She wanted to run away, but she called out, "Is anyone in there? Do you need help?"

There was a moment of silence, broken by clicking and clacking. Papi would say it meant the cabin was settling.

"Yes!" a voice finally exclaimed from behind the door. Whoever was on the other side was talking through the small gap. Vanesa saw a faint glow at the bottom of the door as if the person were swiping a flashlight back and forth.

"Bryce, is that you?" Vanesa asked.

There was some unintelligible talking.

"What?" Vanesa asked again.

She hoped it wasn't a ghost.

"Yes, it's me, Bryce! I'm locked in!" Bryce finally called.

"You mean, 'it is I,'" Emma corrected him.

Vanesa couldn't believe Emma would think about grammar at a time like this. "Guys!" Vanesa yelled over her shoulder to the group upstairs. "I found Bryce!"

The sound of running feet was the only answer.

Eric was the first to arrive, holding a candle. Beck followed closely behind, holding Hunter's hand. Rocky was next, padding down carefully, swaying a little on his feet. Could dogs get baggy eyes from tiredness? Because Rocky looked like he wasn't sure yet whether he was dreaming. He yawned widely, passing the yawn onto Hunter.

Emma and Eric tried to pretend they didn't care about each other, but they didn't fool anyone. They stood side by side, both with crossed arms.

Hunter asked, "Where is he?"

Vanesa pointed at the door. "In there. I think he's trapped."

A rapping sound broke the silence. Hunter visibly shivered.

"I thought it was the ghost of Annabeth," he whispered. "Beck said she trapped trespassers who hunted in her land. Did she trap Bryce in there?"

Vanesa glared at Beck. She'd been scaring Hunter with tales!

Rocky barked twice, and Vanesa didn't get to give Beck another piece of her mind. The barking echoed in the small space of the basement. Then Rocky made his way to the door and scratched it. He whined, looked at Vanesa with begging eyes, and lay in front of it.

Chapter Fifteen
The Hunt for Jolly Ranchers 2.0

Swaggering like a superhero, Eric made his way to the metal door. He pushed it with his shoulder, but of course the door wouldn't budge. It was solid. Built to resist the apocalypse. Or the snowpocalypse in this case.

Vanesa joined Eric next to the gap in the door and called, "Bryce, it's Vanesa!"

"Which one was Vanesa? The one with purple hair?"

"Seriously?" Emma exclaimed behind Vanesa. Vanesa understood why. They looked completely different. The hair was a small detail, but that was what he remembered?

"I'm the one with the black jacket. But it doesn't matter, anyway. What's in there?"

"The bunker!" Bryce yelled, his voice muffled.

Eric looked at the rest of the kids and shrugged. "What bunker?"

"The book said that when they were remodeling the cabin, they found a bunker," Beck explained in her annoying know-it-all voice. "It's a storage room now. Bryce must have gotten trapped when he went in to get the supplies. The door has power locks." She pointed at the keypad on the wall.

"But the power went out *before* he went looking for supplies," Vanesa said.

Beck huffed. "How should I know how he got locked in?"

Vanesa opened her mouth to snap back, but Hunter cut her off. "What's a bunker?" he asked.

"It's a room for when things go all wrong in the world, like in a zombie apocalypse," Beck said, butting into the conversation. Again. "You can lock yourself in, be safe, and wait it out."

Emma and Eric clasped each other's hands. Hunter scurried to hide his face against Vanesa and whimpered.

"Zombies, Vane?" Hunter asked. "Are they coming?"

Vanesa glared at Beck again and said to Hunter, "Don't pay attention to her, Huntercito. She doesn't know anything."

Beck sat on the stairs and bowed her head, hiding her face with a sweep of hair. Rocky moved next to her and laid his head on her feet. She stretched out a hand and ruffled the dog's fur. Any affection Vanesa was starting to feel for the dog vanished, seeing their connection.

Vanesa turned back to the door. "Bryce, how did you get trapped?" she asked.

"I got locked in. Which is practically impossible, but I did. I admit it." There was so much shame in his voice, Vanesa felt bad for him.

"It wasn't the ghost?" she asked.

Emma and Eric held their breaths. Bryce didn't respond.

"Bryce," Vanesa encouraged him.

"Please don't say that!" Bryce sounded like Eric had a moment ago. Terrified. "No, it wasn't the ghost."

Vanesa didn't press him. For now, it didn't matter how he'd locked himself in. What mattered was finding a way to get him out.

"Listen, how do we get you out?" she asked.

"There are two ways out from here," he said. "This main door, which only opens with a code that doesn't work

without electricity or with a key. The second is a secret passageway that I can't find. I've wondered about it since I was
a little boy, but I don't know where it is."

"But how did you get stuck? Where's the key?" Vanesa
asked.

"Well . . . you see . . . I did have the key to this door. I
was keeping it safe, but now I can't find it. I must have
dropped it with my walkie on the way to the cabin. I came
in here when the door was already open—to get the sleeping
bags and the tent, but then I started looking for the ham
radio. A draft closed the door. I know it's dumb. I get it. You
can laugh."

But none of them laughed. Vanesa hadn't made the same
mistake as Bryce, but she'd made other mistakes that turned
out equally bad. She'd failed to protect her brother, and she
was never forgiving herself for that.

And had it really been a draft or had something—
someone—else closed the door?

But thinking about the draft, she remembered something
her mom had told her once.

"My mom went to college here in Utah," Vanesa said, studying the door.

Eric and Emma looked at her with matching confused expressions.

"Too bad intelligence isn't transferable," Beck said, and the smirk on her face looked so familiar, Vanesa searched in her mind for where she knew Beck from. She couldn't remember.

"Actually," Emma said, "intelligence *is* inherited through your mom."

Vanesa mouthed a thank-you to Emma and continued, "*As I was saying*, here in Utah a lot of houses have a basement with a separate entrance. Maybe there's a third exit, one outside that we can open to let Bryce free. Plus, we need the supplies he was getting for us: the sleeping bags and the tent. It's so much colder." Her hands were frozen, and Hunter's teeth were chattering.

"Don't forget the candy," Hunter said. He coughed into his elbow. The hacking sound pierced Vanesa's heart. His throat must hurt so much! "Jolly Ranchers are my favorite," Hunter added in a small voice.

"Is there another door to the outside?" Vanesa called to Bryce.

"I don't know! Let me check." They heard his footsteps and a muffled *ow*. Vanesa and Emma glanced at each other nervously. But just a few moments later, Bryce seemed to come back. "I found it! There *is* another door that looks like it could lead outside!"

Vanesa smiled, feeling a flush of relief. "We can try from the outside."

Bryce tapped on the door furiously. "If it won't open from in here, it won't open from outside!" he shouted. "Don't leave the cabin, guys!"

A little voice in Vanesa's head wondered if it really was a good idea to go outside, even if they stayed close by the kids' lodge. Was Bryce right? Was there any chance they *could* open it from outside? Hunter coughed again.

"We have to try," Vanesa said at last.

"It's pitch-dark out there," Eric said. "I'm not going."

Beck bit her lip and looked away from Vanesa. She didn't need to say there was no way she'd come along. Finally, Emma sighed again and said, "We have to get Bryce out, and it's not going to happen from here. I volunteer as tribute with you. Lead the way."

"But you can't take a candle," Eric warned his sister. "They get blown out with a simple breath. Imagine them out there with the wind."

Vanesa was ready to risk it on her own. She had a feeling that breaking Bryce out of the storage room was the right thing to do.

And then Beck spoke up, extending her phone in one hand. "Here, guys. Take my phone."

"It doesn't work," Emma said.

Beck replied, "The flashlight works."

Vanesa hesitated, standing between a friend and an enemy. What if when she tried to grab the phone, Beck pulled it away? But one look at Hunter's blue-tinged lips convinced her.

"Thanks, Beck," Vanesa said. It was so hard for the words to come out, but her mom's nagging voice in the back of her head told her to mind her manners. "Guys, watch my brother. We'll be right back."

Hunter looked up and grabbed her arm. "Don't leave, Vane. What if the ghost traps you, too? What will I do?" His voice was small and scratchy, and when she held his little hands in hers, they felt so hot and dry. Now Vanesa was even more determined to go out to let Bryce free. The ham radio might be in the storage room! She at least had to try.

Eric had dragged Emma by the arm to a nearby corner and was whispering furiously that she was making a terrible decision. "I won't come looking for you!" he told his sister.

Vanesa couldn't hear Emma's answer. Instead, she knelt down and looked into Hunter's eyes. "I promise I'll come back as soon as possible," she said. "Wait for me by the window, but bundle up. Don't catch a cold." A draft blew down to the basement as if teasing Vanesa. Even if Hunter didn't catch a cold, the cold would catch him.

She brushed her hands over her arms to warm herself up. She looked down at Beck's phone to make sure it still didn't work. The NO CONNECTION banner was the most disappointing sight in the world.

Chapter Sixteen
Whiteout

Eric blocked the front door. "I don't care if you think I'm acting like a baby," he said, spreading his arms so they couldn't go past him. "I'm not letting this happen."

"Eric," Beck said. "We need to help Bryce."

Hunter coughed again, and for a millisecond, Eric got distracted.

Emma took the chance to push him away. "Listen, Eric. Do you want to spend our birthday here in the middle of nowhere? Our lucky twelfth that we've been waiting for all our lives?"

He shook his head and wiped his eyes angrily. Hunter walked up to him and held his hand. "Don't cry, Eric," Hunter said. "My sister will do anything to get us back to the main lodge. She needs to get her phone, you see?"

Vanesa felt a pang of hurt but didn't contradict him. Now that Eric was out of the way, she wanted to make a run for it. She tried to open the door, but the wind was super strong. The snow had piled up so high, it was better at blocking the door than Eric. Much better. The kids gasped.

"Holy amazing!" Eric said, gawking at the snow. "If we stay here a few more hours, the whole cabin will be buried!"

Emma stood next to him and said, "See, Eric? We need to get the sleeping bags and the tent to keep warm. Imagine poor Bryce, locked in the storage room."

Eric's face softened, and he moved to let them pass. "Be careful, please," he said.

"Let's get out quickly so the warm air doesn't escape!" Vanesa called. She was the first one to slither out through the small gap. Since she didn't have her jacket, she'd wrapped herself in blankets. Emma followed her, also wrapped in blankets and wearing Eric's beanie.

Rocky barked twice. He wanted to come along, too.

Vanesa and Emma grabbed the edge of the door and pulled with all their might. The door only moved a couple more inches, but it was enough to get Rocky through. He leapt over Vanesa's feet and took the lead. Emma closed the door behind them.

Vanesa couldn't tell if it was still snowing or if the wind was blowing snow in every direction and making the white-out last longer. Vanesa couldn't see anything but whiteness surrounding them, as if the small cabin was in its own little world, or even its own universe.

The storm made Vanesa feel small—and yet important, too. She and Emma were the only ones willing to brave it. She was still nervous and unsure if this was a good idea. But they had been the ones to find Bryce, and they would find the other door, too. She grabbed Emma's hand, and they followed Rocky, who seemed to understand what they were trying to do. Where they wanted to go. First, he led them around the perimeter of the cabin, keeping close to the wall so they wouldn't get lost. The cabin didn't feel that big inside, but when Vanesa looked up as they walked around it, it seemed like a castle. The logs fit tightly together like a giant game of Jenga. It was amazing that people could build this kind of structure such a long time ago without modern-day tools—that a woman had built it on her own.

"The flashlight," Emma reminded her.

"Right!" Vanesa took Beck's phone from her pocket. Even though they'd been out in the snow for only a few seconds, her fingers were already so cold she was worried they might soon go numb. There hadn't been spare gloves in the cabin, and although she'd wrapped her hands in a blanket, the cold was too piercing. "We need to hurry," she said, her teeth chattering. The blanket she'd grabbed from one of the couches wasn't thick enough to shield her from the fury of the wind. She fumbled with the billowy fabric as she tried to get to the flashlight on the touch screen. Her fingers were so cold, the screen wouldn't respond to her touch.

"Blow on your fingers," Emma suggested.

Vanesa did, but nothing happened.

Rocky whined, and Vanesa had an idea. At the mere thought of what she was about to do, her heart jumped in her throat. But she needed to leave her fear aside if they were going to find the other entrance.

Channeling Hunter's dog-whisperer voice, she called, "Come here, Rocky!"

Rocky wagged his tail so hard it hit a snow-covered bush and sent snow flying in every direction. If Vanesa hadn't been so cold, she would have laughed at his determined expression. Who knew dogs were so perceptive? He stood next to her as if he understood exactly what she was going to do. She rubbed her hands through his fur, and after a few seconds her fingertips felt warm enough to try the screen again. As soon as her finger touched the screen and slid upward, the flashlight came on.

"Genius!" exclaimed Emma.

"You see? I inherited my mom's genes after all," Vanesa said teasingly, and Emma giggled.

Then Vanesa remembered her manners and patted Rocky's head. "Thank you." She was surprised at how much calmer she felt after petting him.

The terrain sloped down after a line of bushes. The girls had to be careful where they stepped so they wouldn't sprain an ankle. Finally, they turned a corner, and on the side that faced the woods, there was a narrow wooden door hidden behind a bush completely covered with snow.

"Bryce!" Vanesa called, standing as close to the door as possible.

Through the crack of the door, the muffled but distinct voice of the kids' ski instructor exclaimed, "By the light of the seven! Thank you!"

Chapter Seventeen
The Sleepwalker

Hearing his master's voice, Rocky started prancing around the girls like a deer. His happiness was infectious, and with each bounce, he scattered more snow on and around them. Vanesa and Emma laughed, and Rocky, knowing he was the center of attention, started howling to the swirling sky. Vanesa wasn't sure if a pack of wolves or coyotes was howling back or if it was the echo of Rocky's voice, but goose bumps broke out all over her body.

From behind the door, Bryce sounded like he was laughing. Or crying. Vanesa couldn't tell. She didn't understand what he was saying because Rocky was making such a racket.

"Rocky!" she snapped. "Quiet!"

It was like magic. As soon as the word was out of Vanesa's mouth, Rocky stopped mid-howl. His round eyes darted from Vanesa to the door as if he wanted Bryce to undo the hex that had stolen his voice.

"Awesome job, Vanesa!" Emma said, a look of admiration on her face. "You should be a dog trainer!"

In spite of how frozen she was, Vanesa felt her face heat up. She imagined herself as the glowworm doll she had loved when she was little.

Rocky sat at attention, waiting for a sign that he was allowed to continue the celebrations for finding Bryce. Or for guiding the girls to Bryce. Vanesa wasn't fluent in dog-speak yet. She kept a stern face and stepped up to Rocky, who lowered his head in a sign of respect.

"I'm going to talk to Bryce to figure out how to rescue him and get us all back to the main lodge," Vanesa told the dog softly. "I'm freezing out here! I need you to be quiet."

Rocky lay like a sphinx and placed his chin on the ground, looking at her through his eyelashes. In spite of her remaining fear, Vanesa felt a tickle of affection for him.

Emma knelt next to Rocky and snuggled close to him. Her teeth were chattering so fast, Vanesa worried the enamel would crack like in a documentary her dad made her watch once. They had to get back inside, and soon.

"Bryce," she said, speaking through the gap in the door again. "Can you hear me? We found the other door."

"You shouldn't have gone outside, girls!" Bryce said. Vanesa could hardly make out his words, which got snatched away by the wind. "But since you made it . . . Can you try to open it?"

She and Emma pulled at the door handle with all their might, but it wouldn't budge. Maybe coming out here hadn't mattered after all.

Vanesa pointed the flashlight of Beck's phone around the edges of the door, looking for another way to open it. Tucked to one side, behind a bush and almost covered with snow, was a pile of tall things leaning against the wall that looked like—

"Skis!" exclaimed Emma when she saw what Vanesa held in her hands. She jumped to her feet and grabbed the other pair. "We can put them on to ski back around the cabin."

"Or back to the main lodge," Vanesa said, ideas already whirring in her mind.

Emma gave her a thumbs-up.

"Bryce!" Vanesa called through the door. "We can't open it from this side, either!"

"That's all right," he called back, sounding glum. Vanesa pushed her ear up against the crack in the door to hear him. "Thanks for trying. Now, get your butts inside the cabin and stay put! What did I tell you about a blizzard? You could get lost. Rocky!" Bryce called, and Rocky sprang to his feet in attention. Bryce continued, "Take the girls back to the cabin and don't let them go out for anything! As soon as it's safe, Luís or someone from the main lodge will get us."

"But are you okay in there?" Vanesa asked.

"Well, I'd love to go to the bathroom. Sorry. TMI, but it's the truth. I'm . . . okay. Don't worry about me."

Emma called, "But what if we find the keys . . ."

"No, stay put." They lost his next few words to the wind, only hearing ". . . snowmobile keys . . . but it's a whiteout." Then, "Stay put. And stay safe. Read a book. If you guys don't know how to read yet, tell stories. Get to know each other!"

Emma and Vanesa exchanged a look of disbelief.

"Of course we can read!" Emma said. "How old do you think we are?"

"Well, no one knew Morse code. I tried to tell you I was trapped in here."

Aha! So the tapping *had* been Morse code.

Vanesa hesitated, but then she said, "Have you found the radio, Bryce?"

"No, I looked all over the place, but no luck," he replied. "Why?"

She looked at Emma, and after Emma nodded, Vanesa continued, "I think my brother's fever's getting worse. What do we do about that?"

"I have medicine in here," Bryce said. "If only the door wasn't locked! Keep him comfortable. Have him drink water—water cures everything. Now go! You're going to freeze to death!"

"Stay safe, Bryce," Emma said.

"Take care of Rocky!" he said, sounding forlorn even through the door.

Vanesa scratched her head. "Take care of Rocky? Isn't he supposed to take care of us?"

"I know. I know. He's a puppy!" Bryce called back.

"A puppy?" Vanesa asked. Hesitantly, she placed a hand on Rocky's head and said, "We'll protect you, Rocky. Don't worry."

Rocky walked to the door and licked it, and again, something stirred inside Vanesa. She would love it if someone loved her that way.

Without another word, she and Emma snapped on the new skis and started to slide carefully back to the cabin's front door. Instead of going back the way they'd come, they continued around the outside. Vanesa kept a hand on the rough wood, worried she'd lose sight of the cabin if she wandered too far.

Soon, they came across the snowmobile—what had Bryce tried to tell them about it? Vanesa glided over to it. She pushed the buttons and moved the handles, but nothing happened.

Emma pushed on a small lever, and the light came on.

"Let's use this light to see since we can't drive the snow-mobile," Emma said. "You can put the phone away and save the battery. I still can't believe Beck let you take her phone! She's very protective of it, you know?"

Vanesa nodded. Mami always said phones were private, so she understood Beck being protective. And she had to admit that it had been generous of Beck to lend them her phone.

Suddenly, in the middle of the snowstorm, when Vanesa wasn't struggling to remember where she knew Beck and her smirk from, the image of the most famous meme of last summer flashed in her mind. The one Amber and the Darlings had sent her. The one that meant dumb, clueless, horrific—everything bad under the sun and beyond.

"No way!" she exclaimed.

"What?" Emma asked.

Vanesa bit her lip. Her fingers itched to text the Darlings. She'd met the *actual* Sleepwalker, the girl from the funniest video she'd seen in her life. This was something she couldn't keep to herself.

"Do you know Beck from before?" Vanesa asked. Her teeth chattered.

"No," Emma said. "She looks familiar, but I've never met her."

"Maybe not in person," Vanesa said, and swallowed the warning that she shouldn't say anything. "Have you seen the Sleepwalker meme?"

Emma licked her lips. Like Vanesa's, they were painfully chapped. Then her eyes widened. "No way." She shook her head, her face shocked. "Beck's Sleepwalker girl?"

"I don't know. *Maybe* she just looks like the girl in the video," Vanesa said. If she looked through Beck's phone, she might find clues. But no, that would be a terrible violation of trust.

Emma shrugged and said, "*Maybe*. But if Beck isn't actually Sleepwalker, they look more like twins than Eric and I do." She slid ahead on her skis, and Vanesa followed.

The way back was easier now with the light from the snowmobile. Vanesa could actually see her skis cut through the fluffy snow. Too bad they didn't have the snowmobile keys! She wondered if they should go back to turn the lights off, but the snowmobile would surely be like Papi's car. Its lights turned off automatically after a while. Besides, she couldn't wait to be inside. Her feet and hands were so stiff she could hardly feel them. She was so tired.

She looked up in time to see Hunter's tear-stained face in the window. With a speed and strength she didn't know she possessed, she pushed hard and flew the last few feet to the front door.

Chapter Eighteen
Boys Are Complicated

Vanesa didn't even feel the weight of her frozen feet anymore as she stepped off the skis. All she cared about was that Hunter was crying. She shouldn't have left him.

It was that day at her birthday party all over again.

"What happened?" she asked.

Hunter flew into her arms. He sobbed, his face pressed to her chest. He was so warm against her! Too warm. She *was* a walking ice sculpture, but his eyes were shiny and his lips had a chalky look, as if he'd put on the sticky lip balm Mami kept in her purse year-round.

"Shhh," she whispered in his ear. "I'm here. I'm here."

The candles flickered with the wind coming in from outside, and she moved out of the way so Emma could shut the door behind them.

Hunter finally looked up at her through his tears. "I was worried you'd left without me. What took you so long? We heard all these noises, and I thought the ghost got you because Eric said—"

"*What?*" Vanesa asked, drilling Eric with her eyes. "For real? Why would you scare a little boy?"

Beside her, Emma was rubbing her feet, which looked dangerously red. Emma couldn't have frostbite, now, could she? And if Emma's feet looked like that, then Vanesa's would look kind of the same. No wonder they throbbed so painfully.

"Listen," she told Hunter. "We found the other door. But we couldn't open it. Bryce is still stuck."

"It *was* him then!" Eric exclaimed, the smile coming back to his face. "I was so scared because of the tapping."

"It was he," Emma corrected, and Vanesa's heart went out to Eric.

"He was trying to communicate in Morse code. Emma was right," Vanesa said.

"So he's still in there? We can't get any help?" Beck asked. Her perma-smirk looked even more familiar now that

Vanesa had made the connection to Sleepwalker girl. Vanesa blinked to erase the image from her eyes. It couldn't really be Beck, could it?

"He lost the keys and all the locks are power locks," Emma answered. "He said not to panic. To stay warm."

But how? The only blankets they had were now soaked and cold with snow. No one but Hunter even had a jacket.

Emma was grimacing with pain.

"Is there a bathroom here?" she asked. "If I can take a hot shower, I might feel better. My feet and my hands feel dead."

Beck nodded. "Yeah, there's a bathroom. We went exploring."

"You did?" Vanesa asked. "In the dark?"

Beck looked taken aback. "Sure, we did. Why would you ask like that?" Then, as if hearing how defensive she sounded, she crossed her arms like a protective shield and said, "Whatever. Yes. We went upstairs and found a bathroom and another room."

"We didn't go to the attic, though," Eric said.

"It might be a portal," Hunter said, and hid his face against Vanesa.

"At least we're not all by ourselves," Beck said. "I mean, there's an adult in the cabin."

"Adult? Bryce must be fifteen. At most," Emma pointed out.

"He has a real job, so he has to be sixteen, right?" Beck argued.

"Um, yes, but he's locked in the basement," Vanesa said, sure that Beck would drop it now.

But no such luck. "*I* feel safer knowing someone is in charge—technically," Beck declared.

"Whatever," said Emma. "I'll feel safer once I get warm. Where's the bathroom? I feel like I'm catching a cold."

Beck sighed dramatically and said, "Come on. I'll show you. It's old-fashioned, but it's clean. There's hot water, and there are new hotel towels. Maybe Bryce sleeps in this cabin when he's on duty."

"No way!" Vanesa said. "He was terrified of spending the night here with—"

"The ghost?" Hunter asked.

Vanesa wanted to smack herself. "No, Huntercito. It's because he . . ." Her mind blanked. Her muddled, frozen brain couldn't find a reason, so she blurted out, "He's a sleepwalker, you see? If he changes his sleep routine, who knows what trouble he'll get into!"

A deadly silence fell over the room. Even the candles stopped flickering as if they, too, were shocked at Vanesa's words. Then Vanesa realized what she'd said: *sleepwalker.* The meme!

After a few seconds, Beck stomped away, and Emma sent Vanesa a look that clearly said *I can't believe you said that.*

Vanesa wanted to take the words back, but it was too late. Even if Beck wasn't the girl from the video, she'd be tired of people thinking that she was. Why did Vanesa always say the wrong thing?

"Wait for me!" Eric exclaimed, clueless as to what had happened. He'd been on the floor with Rocky, who looked untouched by the cold.

"I have to go to the bathroom. Wait here, Eric," Emma said.

Vanesa recognized her tone of voice, and when she looked back at Eric, she saw that the glow on his face from when the girls showed up had vanished. Emma talked to Eric the same way Vanesa talked to Hunter. Poor Eric. He was right. Emma treated him like a baby.

Not that she would say that to him. She didn't want the twins to start fighting again. But she hoped that when Hunter grew, he didn't start hiding his feelings like Eric was doing now.

"Come on, Hunter," Vanesa said, leading her brother upstairs. "Let's use the bathroom after Emma is done."

Hunter sniffed again and wiped his nose with his long sleeves, and although it was gross, Vanesa didn't say anything.

When they reached the landing of the upper floor, Vanesa looked around, but there was no sign of Beck. Emma was in the bathroom. The yellow light of a candle flickered under the door. The sound of the shower was like music to Vanesa's ears. Her whole body ached, especially the leg she'd hurt earlier when she fell from the chairlift. She sat on the pelt that served as a carpet, and Hunter snuggled close to her and finally lay in her lap.

She was horrified to hear that he was wheezing already, the gurgly sound noticeable as he gasped for air in the dry room. The climb up the stairs had been brutal for him, but he hadn't made a peep.

Rocky took a look at Hunter and then Vanesa. In the dog's eyes, Vanesa saw that he could also sense Hunter was in danger.

Chapter Nineteen
Doppelgänger?

Vanesa counted her brother's breaths and studied how long it took him to let each one out. By the way his throat was constricting, she knew that, with each passing second, he was making a greater effort to take a breath. The air was too dry. He'd been too cold without proper winter wear. He was stressed. Maybe he had a small virus, which for Hunter would turn into something more serious soon. She rubbed his back and sang, "Sana, sana, colita de rana," like Mami did when they were sick or hurt.

Hunter's shoulders relaxed at the sound of the familiar tune, but he needed more than a song. Vanesa *had* to get him back to Mami and Papi. But outside, the storm was still raging. The blowing wind sounded like giants laughing at a pillow fight, scattering whiteness all over the world.

Emma came out of the bathroom enveloped in a fluffy bathrobe, looking warmed up.

"The bathrobe was in one of the cabinets," she said, pointing above the sink as Vanesa and Hunter stepped inside the bathroom. "There's a few more if people want to be cozy." She leaned in and whispered, "Why would you say anything about the Sleepwalker in front of Beck?"

Vanesa's cheeks flamed. She tugged at her bracelet, which was fraying already, and avoided Emma's eyes. Luckily the bathroom was in semidarkness, and the mirror was all fogged up from the steam, so she couldn't see the reflection of her embarrassed face. Emma didn't linger and headed downstairs. A tendril of steam followed her.

"Steam!" Vanesa whispered, excited. Bryce had said water could heal anything, and he'd been right! What was steam but water in a different state?

When Hunter's cough sounded doggish, like this, and when he didn't like doing breathing treatments with the nebulizer, Mami would run the hot water in the shower. She'd have Hunter sit on the floor watching a show or playing *DragonVille* on his tablet while he breathed in the steam without realizing it.

This was what Hunter needed now!

Hunter's eyes were heavy with exhaustion, and his lips had a grayish tint that made Vanesa's breath catch in her throat. She held the breath for an uncomfortably long beat. What would it be like for Hunter to live like this every day? She had to get him back to the lodge. How she missed Mami and Papi!

If only the storm stopped. If only someone came to rescue them.

If only . . .

She didn't have the luxury of time to wait. She needed to act.

"Guys! I need help," she called out downstairs.

Silence was the only answer until soft footsteps announced a presence. Vanesa looked quickly over her shoulder, worried it would be the ghost. But it wasn't Annabeth, just Beck, who was so pale, she could almost pass as a ghost herself. She stood next to Hunter, shaking as if she'd gone out into the snow, too.

Vanesa's embarrassment came back in full force. She'd promised she'd never accept help from Beck, and now she had to eat her words.

"I need to make a little bed for Hunter in the bathroom."

Beck nodded. "I know. He needs steam."

Of course, she knew everything, but Vanesa didn't argue this time. Her brother came first.

"Yes, Vane," Hunter said. "A steambath!" His little valentine of a mouth curved into a smile.

Beck seemed to melt at the adorable look on Hunter's face.

"Let me run the water. You make a bed out of towels, Beck," Vanesa said. "Let's hurry so we can close the door and trap the air."

Vanesa turned on the faucet and put the plug in the bathtub. The light-blue ceramic tub was spangled with droplets left over from Emma's shower. She let the hot water run over her cold fingers, and they tingled painfully as they got warmer. Her feet throbbed as if shouting *What about us?*

"Come here, Hunter. I made you a nest," Beck whispered, gesturing to the makeshift bed of towels she'd created on the floor.

Hunter's eyes flickered, like he couldn't keep them open. He coughed again.

Vanesa dried her hands quickly on a towel and helped Beck walk Hunter to the makeshift bed. Rocky lay next to him, and soon, Hunter was snuggled against the dog's tummy. His hair curled on his forehead. Beck sat down with her back against the door.

Vanesa thought about sitting next to her brother, but he looked too warm. The fever would only get worse if he didn't cool down. She unzipped his sweatshirt and took it off. "Let's make sure he puts it back on before he walks out of the bathroom."

"Yeah, so he doesn't get a chill," Beck said.

"Right," Vanesa replied.

Her feet still throbbed, but her fingertips burned like they were on fire. How long had she been outside? She remembered she still had Beck's phone in her pocket. She took it out and handed it back to Beck.

"Thank you for this," Vanesa said. "It saved our lives."

She still had a bad feeling when she thought of the snowmobile. Should they have left the lights on? Now it was too late to go back to turn them off. She couldn't leave Hunter alone again.

Beck took her phone and looked at it sadly. "Too bad it doesn't have a signal yet."

Vanesa studied the older girl. Even with all their disagreements, Beck was here, helping with Hunter. Was she trying to be nice to Vanesa, or doing it for her cute little brother, charmed like everyone always was?

Hunter coughed. It sounded better than it had a few minutes ago, although it still reminded Vanesa of Rocky's barks.

"He used to cry when he had that barking cough when he was littler," Vanesa told Beck. "He was scared he was turning into a dog. Like the movie *The Shaggy Dog*, remember that? But then our abuela got a puppy, and he loved that silly dog, Coco. Then he really wanted to be a dog and wasn't scared of the cough anymore. Now it's just the rest of us who're scared for him." Vanesa brushed the hair off his forehead. Her hand was still too cold, though, and Hunter flinched.

"Sit on the tub," Beck suggested, pointing with her head.

Vanesa was horrified. "Get in the tub with you and Hunter and even Rocky here? Never!"

"On, not *in!*" Beck said in a perfect imitation of Emma, and laughed. It was the first time she'd laughed in front of Vanesa, and it was a wonderful sound. A cross between a snort and a giggle, like the promise of a well of happiness that wanted to be let out.

"What do you mean, then?" Vanesa asked.

Beck wiped the tears off her face—seriously, had it really been that funny? "Sit on the edge of the tub and put your feet in the water. You'll warm up the same as if you've taken a bath." The sparkle was still in her eyes, but there was a touch of sadness in her voice that reached all the way to Vanesa. *But why?* Vanesa wondered.

Vanesa did as Beck suggested. The shock of the water hurt as if the water had been cold instead, but after a couple of heartbeats, Vanesa let out a sigh of relief. "This is awesome. Thanks."

There was a moment in which the only sounds were the voices of Emma and Eric from downstairs. Vanesa couldn't tell if the twins were laughing or arguing.

"I hope they're not fighting," Vanesa said.

Beck gave a little shrug.

Sighs and deep breaths coming from Rocky and Hunter, both asleep, echoed against the walls. Vanesa wanted to break the silence, but she was scared of what to ask Beck. What to say. She didn't even have candy to breach the distance. She only had her words, and those usually led to trouble.

Beck spoke first. "I'm sorry I lashed out at you the first time we met. I was frustrated already and . . . I shouldn't have exploded that way. I'm sorry. Do you have any more pink candy? Pink everything's actually my favorite."

"I noticed," Vanesa said, making a sweeping gesture over Beck's outfit of a pink sweatshirt and pink pants. "But I have no more candy. Sorry."

Beck smiled as if the *sorry* about not having candy covered Vanesa's other mistakes. The truth was, Vanesa was surprised by Beck's apology, by her vulnerability. She was so cool and composed and acted like she didn't care what anyone thought of her. But at the same time she could apologize when she was wrong. How did she get to be that way? Was it because Beck was older? Would one year be enough time for Vanesa to change and be more like Beck—minus the attitude? It didn't seem possible—not when her hands and brain were going through withdrawal from not checking in with the Sunshine Darlings or worrying that Amber would treat her like trash for not following the group's rules.

"It's okay," Vanesa finally said. "I'm sorry that I crashed into you, and then said that about your mom, and then made you fall, and called you a porcupine, and I said that thing about . . ." Now that she listed all the things she'd done, she was shocked Beck was even talking to her. If Vanesa were closer to the candle, she'd have caught on flames of embarrassment.

Beck looked at her as if waiting for a bomb to explode, and Vanesa bit her lip while she recited in her head *You won't mention the meme. You won't mention the meme. You won't . . .*

"Said that thing about what?" Beck asked, her voice resigned, like she wanted to deal with whatever Vanesa was thinking.

Vanesa wanted to run away, but she couldn't. Hunter was breathing a little better. She didn't want to wake him yet, and she couldn't leave him alone. She turned the water off, though, so the bathtub wouldn't overflow. While she did, she composed herself and planned how to respond to Beck.

"I feel like I've seen you before . . . ," Vanesa said at last. "Online. But it must be that you have a famous dopple . . . dopple . . . I forget the word," she said.

The sparkle went out of Beck's eyes. She sighed. Her shoulders slumped unfashionably. She had a sweet crooked smile. "Doppelgänger? Twin? Vanesa, are you talking about the girl from that Sleepwalker video last summer?"

"Yes," Vanesa said. She felt breathless.

"How long have you known?"

Vanesa didn't know how to answer, and Beck, sensing her hesitation, said, "It doesn't matter. But, yes, the girl in the Sleepwalker meme is me. Or, like Emma would say, that girl is I."

Chapter Twenty
The Other Vanesa

Beck took a long breath, like she was getting ready to jump off a cliff, and went on.

"Last summer, I went to camp for the first time in my life. I wasn't worried, though. I'd never had trouble making new friends. That was before." Beck paused, as if she needed to swallow.

"What happened?" Vanesa asked, her breath still bated.

"Vanessa happened."

Vanesa had to catch herself before she fell in the tub. "Are you serious? Me?"

Beck smiled sadly. "Not you, silly. Another girl named Vanessa. Your name's not that uncommon, you know."

Vanesa shrugged her shoulders. "I'm Vanesa with one *s*. Not that common where I live. By the way, where do *you* live?"

"New York," Beck said. "And you're right. She was—is—Vanessa with two *s*'s."

Vanesa was a little comforted thinking her name wasn't exactly like the other girl's. Whatever she'd done to Beck, it couldn't be good. "So what happened?" she asked.

"At camp, Vanessa and I became best friends instantly. We clicked, you know? We loved the same things." Beck shook her head. "Actually . . . I started forgetting what I loved and pretending I loved what she told me I should love."

Like hating pink? Like not trying out for sports but wanting to cheer instead? Does that ring a bell? Vanesa wished she had a mute button for the voice of her annoying conscience.

"That's dumb," Vanesa said, and then, realizing what she'd said, clapped a hand over her mouth.

Beck didn't seem offended, though. On the contrary, she nodded. "Sure! It was dumb. It is, but I didn't see it. Not for a long time. I was so nervous about making a mistake and that Vanessa would kick me out of her group that I started having nightmares."

Vanesa could tell this wasn't the worst thing yet, and she braced herself for the rest of Beck's story. She'd seen that

Sleepwalker video so many times. It was hilarious. In it, a girl—Beck—sleepwalked alone in the dark, with the now-familiar smirk on her face, looking pleased with herself. But then she woke just as she tripped into the pool, and through a screen, the look of shock on the girl's face was so funny. But now Vanesa was horrified that she'd laughed at all.

Beck's cheeks were bright red. "I've never told anyone about this . . . I'm not sure . . . But you remind me of the other Vanessa, and I never got to tell her how much she hurt me." Beck paused. "If you tell . . ."

"I won't tell anyone," Vanesa said, lifting her hand, palm facing out, as if she were taking an oath. "I promise."

The gesture must have been enough for Beck because she said, "On top of the nightmares, I started sleepwalking. One night, I woke up next to the pool, and I got so panicked that I fell in. I couldn't even swim. It turns out the whole camp knew I sleepwalked because Vanesa was recording me and posting it on her social media story every night. I had no idea. But people were making bets on how long it would go on before I found out. They—she—made memes about me, and one of them—the one of me falling into the pool—went viral."

Beck laughed but wiped the tears running down her face. "That's when the anxiety started. When I got home, I couldn't go to sleep for days and days. I was scared of the dark. I still am . . ."

"How did you get through it all?" Vanesa asked.

Beck shrugged. "I'm stubborn, I guess."

Vanesa carefully got her feet out of the tub. She dried them and then sat next to Beck and patted her hand. Her first impulse was to give her a hug, but Beck still had a human porcupine vibe; she didn't seem like a huggable kind of person. What Vanesa felt more strongly was that Beck needed to talk to bring out the hurt that she'd kept inside for so long.

Vanesa knew that it wasn't fun to cry or express herself when she was sad, but it was worse to keep those feelings inside, where they'd fester. If that happened, then those tears hurt even more. Beck had shared so much. Vanesa wanted to show that she could be supportive and that they could put all their arguments behind them.

And she wouldn't tell anyone about Beck, not even Amber, who'd turn green with envy if she knew Vanesa had met her. Vanesa remembered that she'd already told Emma what she suspected about Beck's identity. She opened her mouth to tell Beck in case Emma mentioned something and Beck got the wrong idea. In that moment, though, Rocky's ears perked. He whined in his sleep, as if he were answering a call only he could hear. He woke, jumped to his feet, and faced the girls, as if asking them to please move out of the way.

Vanesa and Beck moved to let him out, right as Emma yelled from downstairs like her soul was being ripped from her body.

Beck opened the bathroom door, and Rocky darted toward the sound of distress. The girls looked at each other with alarm, and they followed Rocky.

Chapter Twenty-One
SOS

They rushed downstairs, and Vanesa imagined the worst: Eric had choked on popcorn or fallen off the couch and broken his arm. The ghost had spooked Emma or her fingers were frostbitten after all, and they'd fallen off or . . . Vanesa couldn't think what else could've happened for Emma to yell like that.

But it wasn't a ghost or any of the other terrible things Vanesa had imagined. Emma and Eric faced each other, mirror images of hurt and annoyance. They were yelling at each other at the top of their lungs. Eric had a vein throbbing in his throat, and when Emma replied, spit flew out of her mouth. Eric either didn't notice or he didn't want to take an extra breath to tell her how disgusting it was.

Beck looked at Vanesa like she didn't know what to do. Should they get between the fighting twins? Should they get involved at all?

Vanesa stepped between them and said, "Guys! You have to stop fighting! My mom always says that when siblings fight against each other, the outsiders eat them up, or something like that. It sounds better in Spanish."

Out of the corner of her eye, she noticed a handheld game on the couch. The image of a destroyed *DragonVille* village flickered on and off. Vanesa knew enough about the game to know that whoever was playing hadn't paid attention to the raiding party's approach . . . or the batteries were dying. Without power or access to batteries, next time Eric or Emma logged on, they wouldn't have a village at all.

"You lied to me," Emma was saying to her brother. "You went behind my back and planned another party with boys! Why? Because you think I'm not good enough for you anymore?"

Eric shook his head and pressed his lips, his eyes darting to Beck and Vanesa, who were watching their reactions like spectators at a tennis match. "Of course not," he said.

"Liar!"

"Yeah, I found a new group of friends, but not because I think you're not good enough," Eric said.

"Then why?" Emma demanded, her hands on her hips as she tapped her foot on the floor.

Once he made sure no one's life was in mortal danger, Rocky sleepily headed back upstairs. To be with Hunter, Vanesa guessed, and her heart swelled with emotion for the slobbering beast.

"Because you're the one who thinks you're better than me, Emma," Eric said. "Just because you got your growth spurt before I did and you speak like Shakespeare doesn't mean you're in charge of me, okay? I like *DragonVille* and *Mario*. Is it wrong that I don't like piñatas? Is it a crime? That's all I said and you freaked. I feel like we can't talk anymore. I play with the guys because they don't put me down all the time. You're always pushing me aside. What? You don't want to be part of the twin team anymore?"

Emma shook her head and her beads clinked. "It's not that, Eric. I'm on the twin team for life. The thing is, you keep saying we're halves of a whole. But what if we're two whole people that make a bigger team? I don't want to be a half of anything."

Eric looked at her like they were understanding each other for the first time in forever. "I know. I feel the same way," he said, and Vanesa heard his voice crack. "I'm sad that we're becoming strangers. Like we need to get to know each other all over again. It was so easy when we were little, Em."

Emma stepped toward him and hugged him. Vanesa sighed with relief. She thought the storm inside the cabin had been averted, but then Eric said, "I'm sure that when you discovered my secret gaming bros, I had the same face as Sleepwalker girl." He laughed, but Emma made a warning sign with her hands. She glanced at Beck and back at Eric, frantic for her brother to get the hint.

Eric followed her eyes, and after a few seconds, comprehension dawned on him. "What?" he exclaimed. "Sleepwalker girl is Beck?"

Emma bit her lip and mumbled, "That's what Vanesa said . . ."

Beck looked at Vanesa with so much hurt in her eyes that Vanesa wished the earth would open up and swallow her.

"Beck, wait, I didn't—"

"Save it," Beck growled. "I guess you're just like the other Vanessa after all."

"I didn't tell her!" Vanesa said.

But Emma added, "You did . . ."

Beck's eyes filled with tears and walked away without giving Vanesa the chance to explain that she had told Emma—earlier.

But then, Hunter's little voice called her from upstairs. "Vane! Help me!"

Vanesa ran up the stairs two at a time as if she could escape the hurt she'd seen in Beck's face.

In the bathroom, Hunter sat up, his dark eyes big and surprised to see her. "I was afraid you'd be the ghost!" he said, his chin quivering like when he tried to keep the tears at bay.

"Of course I'm not the ghost, superboy."

He wrapped his arms around her neck and said, "I'm not a superhero. I've only been sleeping . . ." He took a long, shallow, shuddering breath and coughed again. The effort it took her brother to inhale made Vanesa's chest clench.

"I have you," she said. "Now, let's go downstairs slowly." The steam in the bathroom was dissipating because the door had been left open for so long.

"I'm so scared, Vane. Tell me a story," Hunter said.

She peeked outside the bathroom and grabbed a red book of fairy tales from a bookcase. In the portraits on the wall, Annabeth Grant's eyes seemed to follow Vanesa's every move.

Carefully, so she wouldn't slip and bring her brother down with her, Vanesa led Hunter back to the other kids. Beck sat in a chair on her own. Eric and Emma hovered around her, sending furtive looks at Vanesa, as if *she* were now the bad guy in the movie.

The temperature downstairs was way colder than it had been a few minutes ago. Eric's teeth were chattering.

Vanesa helped Hunter onto the sofa. Rocky lay down next to Hunter, unwilling to leave his side.

"It's too cold for Hunter," Vanesa said. How long could they stay this cold?

Nobody responded, and Vanesa sat next to her brother, listening with dread to how labored his breath was.

Then the tapping started again.

This time, the message was obvious.

Three short taps followed by three long ones and then three more short ones.

"It means SOS," Hunter said, gasping for breath. "He's calling for help."

Chapter Twenty-Two
The Portrait's Secret

"We need to find a way to get Bryce out of that room," Vanesa said. "He must be freezing." Even by the struggling candlelight, she could see the steam of her breath.

"I'm worried about him, Vane," Hunter said.

The rattling in his throat was worse than ever.

How long had they been here? The night felt endless, especially with Hunter's rough breathing and her misunderstanding with Beck. They'd been so close to making up.

And if something happened to Hunter, how would Vanesa ever tell Mami and Papi that she'd been too scared to rescue them herself? Especially when they shouldn't have been here to start with.

Vanesa got to her feet. It was time to make a plan.

"Beck," Vanesa said softly. Maybe she could help Beck feel better if the other girl had something to do. "Why don't you read to Hunter from this book?" Vanesa held out the fairy-tale volume she'd found upstairs.

Beck glared, but she did take the book from her.

As Beck began reading Hunter a story, Vanesa listened again to Bryce's tapping. And then she remembered: Bryce *had* said there was another way to the storage! How had she forgotten his mention of a secret passageway? She knew it had to be real. Mami had told her of her days discovering secret passages with her roommates in college. There had to be another passageway to the storage room. Vanesa was sure of it.

She needed to find it.

"Eric," Vanesa said. "Would you lend me your boots? They're drier and warmer than mine. I'm going to try to get Bryce. I think he has the keys for the snowmobile. That's our best chance to get back to the main lodge."

"But we already tried outside, Vanesa," Emma said. "We can't get him out."

"There's another way into the storage room. I'm sure of it."

Eric shrugged and took off his boots without complaining. "Good thing my feet are bigger than Emma's or they wouldn't fit you."

"They're smellier than mine, so poor Vanesa," Emma said. Vanesa could tell she was teasing Eric out of habit. There wasn't a hint of meanness in her voice.

Vanesa put on the boots and wrapped herself with one of the smaller blankets, damp from when she went out in the snow.

"Be careful, Vane," Hunter said. "Are you scared?"

She smiled. "I have a guardian angel. Come here, Rocky," she said, and Rocky snapped to attention. "Let's get your Bryce."

She set off upstairs to the attic, and Rocky followed her gingerly, his nails click-clacking on the hardwood. Vanesa hummed a song that her mom used to sing to her when she was scared. It was true that she didn't have anyone with her now to tell her where to go or what to do, but she had a voice inside telling her that she at least was trying, and that was enough.

She reached the upstairs room, wondering if the book-shelves hid anything. In an old movie she'd seen, there'd been a secret passageway behind a bookshelf.

She felt a chill slide around her and shivered, imagining Annabeth watching her. But the chill wasn't her imagination. She followed a hissing draft to a little door in the wall. Holding her breath, Vanesa carefully creaked it open. The attic. She took a deep breath and got on her knees. She crawled into the tiny space, dust and spiderwebs grabbing at her, and when she stood up, she pawed them off her arms. When she turned, she found herself face-to-face with a large, terrifying painting. Rocky, who'd followed her, whined and hid his face with his paw. Did he sense something ghostly in the air?

"Hello, Annabeth," Vanesa whispered.

Annabeth didn't reply, thankfully. If she had, Vanesa would've fainted.

Annabeth sure had a lot of paintings of herself. And this painting looked like it belonged in a castle or museum. It was majestic. It showed Annabeth dressed in men's clothes, like a cowboy, her short hair curling around her ears. Her square jaw and brown eyes made her look menacing in the small attic space. But Vanesa swore she could almost see a smile in the woman's eyes.

The cold draft, like a breath, was coming from underneath the painting.

Vanesa felt a thrill of realization. The draft didn't mean the cabin was haunted. It meant there was an opening on the other side!

The painting was heavy, but Vanesa pulled with all her might. When she was about to give up, the frame moved. And there it was: an opening. A secret passageway!

Wow.

The opening led to a rickety wooden staircase. A faint light glowed from the bottom of the stairs. Without hesitating, Vanesa stepped in and headed down the steps, calling for Bryce. Rocky followed close behind.

No one answered, but she kept going down. The staircase was a swirl. She got dizzy, and then she crashed into a wall of empty boxes. She pushed them aside and saw a sleeping bag and scattered candy wrappers. She was there—in the storage room.

"Bryce?" she called softly.

Rocky whined, and a voice from behind the boxes asked, "Rocky? Is that you, boy?"

For a second, Vanesa thought it might be fun to scare Bryce and pretend she was Annabeth, but the poor boy had been alone in the storage room for a long time.

"Bryce, it's me. Vanesa. I found a way out!" she called.

Gingerly, Bryce walked out from behind the boxes. He was shivering. Vanesa didn't know if it was from fear or cold. Maybe a combination.

"Thank goodness!" Bryce exclaimed, his hands up in the air like he was praying. "I knew one of you girls would rescue me! You're plucky people!"

Rocky bounded to his master and covered him in slobbery kisses. This time, Vanesa didn't gag.

"Bryce," she said. "Hunter needs a doctor. He's not doing too well." Now that she said her fear aloud, her throat closed up. She couldn't cry. Not now. So she bit her lip until the knot in her throat disappeared.

Bryce snapped to attention, and Rocky quickly copied him by sitting still like a statue. The gesture would've been funny under other circumstances.

"Follow me," Bryce said. First, he grabbed some flash-lights, granola bars, and a bag of Jolly Ranchers.

"You have the snowmobile keys, right?" she asked.

He patted his pocket, which jingled. "Right here, madam!"

Then Bryce led her and Rocky back up the winding stair-case and through the secret passage.

When they emerged from the passageway, Bryce looked at Vanesa and asked, "How did you find it? I've heard stories since I was a little boy, but I was too scared to look for it!" He walked ahead of Vanesa, and when they reached the little door, he added, "I don't even want to know," he said.

His eyes glazed right past Annabeth's painting, but Vanesa whispered, "Thank you, Annabeth."

Annabeth smiled like she was happy that Vanesa had found her secret passageway after all these years.

Vanesa followed Bryce downstairs to the main room. Emma and Eric, who'd been sitting on the rug, jumped to their feet when they saw Bryce. Beck was calmly reading to Hunter, but his breathing sounded worse than ever. He needed medical care immediately.

"We'll get you to the main lodge right away, guys," Bryce said.

"The phones are still down," Emma said. "We tried again, but nothing."

"We have the snowmobile," Bryce said. "Come with me, Vanesa. I might need help getting it out of the snowbank, and you already have boots on. Eric, protect the ladies," Bryce said, and then laughed because Eric was huddled as close to Emma as he could. There was no doubt as to who was doing the protecting.

Vanesa and Bryce headed outside, and Vanesa caught her breath. It had been cold before, but Vanesa had only felt it after standing in the snow for a few minutes. Now the effect was instantaneous. It was like walking into a freezer. She'd thought the snow had stopped, but it still fell gently. Her eyelashes curled like when she opened the dishwasher and the steam hit her on the face. How strange that heat and cold had similar effects, even though they were perfect opposites.

The thrill of having found the passage behind the painting evaporated like magic, and Vanesa just focused on trying to keep warm.

She and Bryce trudged along the side of the cabin, stepping on the footprints Emma and Vanesa had made not so long ago. The prints didn't look very deep because it had snowed more, but they were still visible.

When they finally reached the snowmobile, Vanesa could've cried with happiness. Safety was only minutes away.

"We'll have your brother back in an instant," Bryce said. But when he put the key in the ignition, there wasn't a roar of the engine. The weak click was the worst sound in the world. Vanesa knew what it meant even before Bryce exclaimed, "Oh no—the snowmobile is dead!"

Chapter Twenty-Three
A Piece of Runaway Storm Cloud

Vanesa felt the sky falling down on her head. Of course, it was only snow. More snow. Normally, she would have loved it. She'd been so excited to come to Pinecloud Lodge. She'd been so eager to play in the snow. Just like she'd been eager to become a permanent member of the Sunshine Darlings. But instead, she'd gotten herself trapped without a phone when her brother was in mortal danger. He needed his inhaler. He might even need to go to the emergency room by now.

She'd ruined everything.

Bryce shook his head and muttered, "How could the battery have run out? Maybe I left the lights on . . . ? But last time I drove it here, I made sure everything was off."

Vanesa wanted to burrow into the snow and hide until next summer. It had been so easy to walk back to the cabin because of the light from the snowmobile. But now when they needed it for what it was built to do, it didn't work. And it was all her fault. She'd had a feeling in her gut, and she'd ignored it. Abuela Bea would be so disappointed.

"Bryce," she said quickly before she could stop herself. "I turned the lights on after Emma and I came outside to try to get you. I'm sorry."

Bryce looked at her openmouthed, like his words were frozen and he couldn't get them out.

"Is there a way we can jump-start it? Like a car?" she asked, sheepishly.

Bryce's freckles stood out against the paleness of his face. His scraggly hair was matted. "No. It's not like a car. We need to get ahold of the main lodge . . ."

Now it was his time to blush. And Vanesa knew why. If he hadn't dropped his walkie-talkie, then the adults in the main lodge would've known the kids needed help hours ago. Vanesa's heart clenched.

Bryce's teeth were chattering. "Let's go back inside before we catch our deaths," he said, looking at the ominous dark woods. There was a rustle of branches, and for a second,

Vanesa thought she saw the glint of yellow eyes watching them. She shook her head so the thoughts would go away. There were no ghosts out here.

She followed Bryce back to the cabin. Rocky was a shadow in the snow next to them. He must have been able to feel the severity of the situation, and there was nothing he could do.

Inside, Beck was still reading a story aloud, her voice shaky. Emma and Eric watched Hunter with worried expressions.

Rocky whined, voicing what Vanesa was feeling: dark despair at seeing her little brother struggle for each breath.

Bryce announced to the room, "The snowmobile doesn't work."

For a horrible second Vanesa thought he'd tell everyone that it was her fault.

"Even if it did," Bryce added, "we can't go out in the storm yet. It's too dangerous."

Vanesa turned around to hide the gratitude burning her eyes. She'd made so many mistakes, and Bryce was covering up for her! If only she had left the snowmobile alone . . .

She had to fix this mess!

The main lodge was too far for her to walk.

But if she found the walkie-talkie . . .

She thought back to that signpost she'd seen from up near the attic. She just *knew* that shadow had been Bryce's backpack—and the walkie-talkie. That was the key to getting out of here. And she had to follow her instinct.

As if he'd heard her thoughts, Rocky looked at her and nodded.

Maybe she and Rocky had a connection after all. The dog slowly got up from next to Hunter, and silent like a shadow or a piece of runaway storm cloud, he came toward Vanesa.

Bryce was passing out granola bars to the other kids and telling them his ideas for waiting out the whiteout.

But Vanesa had other plans. She could do it; she could save them all. She felt it, and this time, she wasn't ignoring her gut.

"Let's go, Rocky," she said, and Rocky trotted to her side, wagging his tail.

Chapter Twenty-Four
Over and Out

"I'm going to the bathroom," Vanesa told Bryce.

He was in the middle of a story about a rescue team he'd been a part of. Only Hunter seemed mesmerized; the rest of the kids looked sleepy. But Bryce nodded at her and kept talking. Vanesa walked away, and when she looked over her shoulder and saw that no one was watching her, she cracked open the door and slipped out.

The snow fell in bigger chunks. Once she'd heard that when the snowflakes got bigger, it meant that the storm was coming to an end. She hoped that was true.

The pair of skis she and Emma had found waited for her beside the door. She confidently clicked Eric's boots into them and started sliding toward the signpost.

On the inside, though, she was all confusion. Her gut had told her she could do this, that she could save the day.

And yet, all her insecurities yelled that she was making the worst mistake of her life. That she should've stayed put, let Bryce get them out of this problem. Or at least she should have taken someone with her or told someone where she was going. But she'd *seen* the bundle with the walkie-talkie from the upstairs window.

She propelled herself with the poles, and the skis slid softly on the pristine snow that glinted when the moonlight peeked ever so briefly from behind the clouds. Their ski lesson at noon seemed like a lifetime ago. Rocky padded beside her. He looked at her with so much trust it was enough to keep her going. It was enough to reassure her.

She got into the rhythm of moving on the skis, and she kept peering over her shoulder. The kids' lodge was still there. How long until Bryce and the others discovered that she'd left on her own? She quickened her pace, but when she stumbled, she tried to balance herself with open arms.

She saw the signpost with its arrows pointing in every direction.

"Almost there!" she said. She shuffled forward, and when she finally reached the bundle of Bryce's supplies, Vanesa felt vindicated. She knew it'd be here!

Like Abuela Bea had told her—all she had to do was listen to her gut. It was never okay to doubt herself so much that she couldn't understand what her heart was saying. And her heart, the hunch that told her it was Bryce's backpack that she'd seen from the window, hadn't been wrong.

Her hands were stiff. She couldn't flex her fingers. She warmed up her hands in Rocky's fur so she could open the bag. The moon had disappeared back behind the heavy clouds, so she couldn't see what was inside. But her hands rummaged through the contents until, at the bottom, she touched the hard edges of something rectangular and plastic.

She took it out and exclaimed, "The walkie-talkie!"

She jumped in the air, celebrating. If anyone was looking out the window they'd have the time of their lives seeing a wild-haired girl dancing, wrapped in so many blankets that she looked like a yeti.

She unfurled the walkie-talkie's antenna and pressed a button. There was no sound. Vanesa's heart sank. It was the snowmobile all over again.

"Please," she whispered. Her throat hurt. The air was pure and sharp and cut through her nostrils all the way to her lungs as if she were breathing ice. "Please let it work."

She shook it, pushed all the buttons, lowered and extended the antenna. It was all for nothing. The walkie was dead.

This was her last chance to communicate with the world and let the main lodge know that Hunter needed help! That she, Vanesa, wanted to be lying in bed—she didn't care whether it was the sofa bed or the fluffy bed—not stranded alone in a snowdrift.

She wanted to wring her hands in desperation, but she didn't want to drop the walkie-talkie and risk losing it. As if it were a fidget spinner, she turned the dial on top of the walkie.

And static broke the absolute silence.

Even the wind stopped in surprise.

"It works?" Vanesa asked in an exhausted whisper.

Excitedly, she turned the volume dial. She'd been on the wrong channel!

There was another crackle of static, but it got cut off every other second. Vanesa knew she couldn't let the battery die. But she couldn't turn the walkie-talkie off and lose the shaky connection. It was now or never.

"You can do this," she told herself.

Rocky rubbed his head on her leg like a cat. It was his way of saying he trusted in her, too.

She pushed the button and spoke. "Pinecloud Lodge, do you read me?" Was she supposed to say *over* or something? She wasn't sure, so she waited for a reply.

There were a couple of seconds during which her thumping heart overcame the sounds of the night in the woods. But when she was about to lose hope, a scratchy voice spoke back, "This is Pinecloud Lodge. Who's there? Over."

There was no time to celebrate.

Vanesa took a long breath and spoke. "It's Vanesa Campos. We're stranded in the kids' lodge. The power went out, and one of the kids needs medical attention. Over."

There was a flurry of voices in the background, all speaking at the same time, but the one voice that made Vanesa's heart jump to her mouth was Mami's.

"Mi amor, are you guys safe? Oh my gosh, talk to me, Vane!"

Vanesa's hand trembled. She felt overwhelmed by the love in her mom's voice. But Vanesa kept her own voice strong and steady. "I'm fine, Mami, but send help. Hunter needs his inhaler."

"We're on our way, Vane. We're on our way." Papi's voice reverberated in the air, but most of all in Vanesa's mind and heart.

She turned around as fast as she could to tell the kids she'd saved them. But she spun so quickly, forgetting her skis, that she felt her ankle twist with a sharp pain. She fell to the snow with a thud and a loud cry. She tried to untangle the skis beneath her feet, but her ankle hurt too much.

Rocky, who'd sprinted ahead, came back for her. He pawed at the snow impatiently.

"Rocky," she said, her voice cracking. "I need help. Go get help for me."

There was a rustling in some nearby trees.

Rocky's ears perked up, and he turned to look, ears pricked. If he got distracted chasing shadows, no one would know that Vanesa needed help.

"Rocky, listen. Go get help." She pointed toward the dark outline of the kids' lodge.

Rocky dashed out in the opposite direction. Toward the trees.

Vanesa lay in the snow all alone.

Chapter Twenty-Five
Rescue Party

A sob rose in Vanesa's throat, and she let herself cry. She was so cold, she thought she'd never be warm again. Her tears seemed to freeze on her cheeks. So much for following her gut. She'd made a mess of everything. Talk about ruined vacations! Mami and Papi wouldn't ever let her step outside their house next spring break. If she made it. Why hadn't she told anyone what she planned to do?

She pounded on the snow, and her Darlings friendship-promise bracelet snapped off her wrist. It lay on the snow like a dried-up earthworm. Now Amber would kick her out of the group for sure, as if Vanesa's breaking the streak wasn't enough.

But . . . did it really matter?

In spite of the whirlwind of emotions inside her, Vanesa felt . . . free.

No more posts to reply to the second she got them. No more hiding what she really liked so that her *friends* would let her be in the group. If she couldn't be herself with Amber and the Darlings, were they really her friends?

A dog barked in the distance. Was that Rocky—or a coyote or wolf?

The barking got closer and closer, and when she looked up from the torn bracelet, she saw a shadow of a dog, Rocky, and a lone figure skiing in her direction behind him.

Beck reached her before Vanesa had time to compose herself.

"What are you doing here?" Vanesa asked, then realized how unfriendly her voice sounded. She didn't mean to snap at Beck, who'd come to help her in spite of their disagreements.

Beck's familiar smirk appeared. "I had a bad feeling when you said you were going to the bathroom. I heard Rocky barking. I knew you needed help," she said.

Vanesa brushed her hair out of her face to appear more dignified. She wanted to say *yes*, *no*, *thank you*, but the words were frozen inside her. Beck had left the cabin and ventured into the darkness to save her? After what Vanesa had said and done?

Even if you were the only person who knew the way, I wouldn't go with you. Even if you were rescuing me from disaster, I wouldn't follow you anywhere, Rebecca.

As if Beck could read Vanesa's mind, she said, "I thought we could be friends."

Vanesa sighed and poked at the snow with her finger. But Beck had opened up to her, and Vanesa could return the favor. She owed Beck an apology. "I did tell Emma about the meme," Vanesa said, and seeing Beck's eyes fill with tears, she quickly added, "But it was way before *you* told me what had happened. I promise I wouldn't break my promise."

Beck pressed her lips together and looked at Rocky. They stared at each other for a moment as if Beck were consulting the dog. Rocky *had* been with Emma and Vanesa outside during that conversation after all.

Finally, Rocky barked once.

Beck smiled like she understood exactly what he meant and looked back at Vanesa. "I'm sorry I didn't tell Eric and

Hunter about the storm when I saw them leaving," she said. "I never thought it would get this bad."

"I didn't, either," Vanesa said. Her ankle throbbed, and she winced in pain.

Beck knelt down beside her in the snow. "Why did you leave the cabin alone?" Beck asked.

"To find this," Vanesa said, and showed her the walkie-talkie.

Beck's eyes went wide like full moons. "So you decided to take matters into your own hands and be the hero?"

Vanesa started shaking. "I didn't want to play the hero. I was following my gut. I saw Bryce's backpack from the window. I had to get it. For Hunter. But then I got hurt. And here I am, needing your help."

Beck smiled crookedly, but not in a judgy way. "I guess you're a modern-day Annabeth Grant."

Warmth spread inside Vanesa, all the way from her heart until it spilled from her eyes. She pressed Beck's hand and said, "Thank you."

A burst of wind stunned them. Beck was the first one to recover. "Let me help you," she said. "We need to get back."

Vanesa stood on her uninjured leg. She tried to balance, but she couldn't step on her hurt foot. Beck draped her arm around Vanesa's waist, and little by little, they shuffled on the snow back to the kids' lodge. Bryce was waiting for them with a grim expression on his face. Vanesa steeled herself for his reaction, but a beam of light shone on Bryce's face and he squinted. Vanesa looked over her shoulder. The light came through the snow from the distance. From the main lodge.

"We're saved!" said Bryce.

As the light approached, Vanesa realized it was the beam of a pickup truck's headlights. The snowplow on the front of it slowly heaped up drifts to one side. The Pinecloud flag whipped in the wind from the top.

Vanesa couldn't see the faces of the driver and the passenger, but she hoped her parents were in the truck.

Vanesa hobbled inside to get her brother ready. Emma knelt next to Hunter. He was shivering, although he was covered in blankets. The fever had increased. His anxiety at feeling sick had affected his asthma even more.

"Mami is coming, Huntercito," Vanesa told him, brushing his sweaty hair from his forehead.

"You're the best sister a ninja like me could ever want," he whispered, and this time, she didn't care that the whole room could hear his words.

The sun exploded inside Vanesa's heart. It was almost worth the difficulty of the night to hear those sweet words. His lips were so chapped, and she helped him sit up so he could take a sip of water.

"Where are they?" Mami's voice rang from the front door.

"Rebecca! Beck, are you okay?" Beck's mom sounded panicked.

The kids parted to let them through.

Beck ran to her mom's arms, and although Vanesa couldn't hear the sound of her friend crying, Beck's mom whispered, "Shh . . . You're okay now. You guys are okay." Beck's mom wore joggers and a thin, long-sleeved T-shirt as if she'd run out to rescue her daughter without thinking of the cold.

"I know, Mom," Beck replied, her stuffy nose making her sound like she was speaking underwater. "I'm so worried about Hunter, though."

Vanesa's mom reached the little nest the kids had made underneath the table: a fort to protect Hunter from the bitter cold. She wore her heavy furry parka over her pajamas, the ones with bunnies that matched Vanesa's. When Mami saw Vanesa, her eyes lit up, and the expression of anguish and worry vanished at least for a couple of seconds.

"We had no idea, mi amor! We thought you were having a blast here," she said, and hugged Vanesa so tight, she could feel Mami's heart beating wildly.

"He needs his medicine," Vanesa said.

Mami let her go and took something out of her pocket. Vanesa had always thought the inhaler was so ugly. Gray plastic and a bright-blue button on the top. But at the sight of it now, her brother's savior, tears sprang to her eyes.

"Mamita brought you the inhaler, Hunter," Vanesa said, shaking her brother's arm softly so that he'd wake up.

His eyelids fluttered, and he whispered, "About time!"

Everyone laughed, even Rocky, who yelped and bounced so high his nose almost touched the ceiling.

But the best sound was the whoosh of the inhaler when Hunter pressed the button and took the medicine that would help him breathe better. It was like magic. After the first dose, the blue tinge faded from his face as if someone were retouching the color in a photograph. Soon the color returned to his lips and neck. Just like that, the balloon of tension had popped and everyone could breathe better because Hunter could.

"Let's get you back to the lodge," Mami said to Hunter. She looked at Vanesa. "Josiah said he'd have to make two trips bringing you kids because we can't fit you all."

"What time is it?" Vanesa asked.

"Eleven fifty," Mami replied.

"It's almost our birthday!" Emma exclaimed, looking at Eric with a forlorn expression.

Vanesa knew that by the time the truck came back for her, it would be past midnight and her streak would be over. She'd ruin the Darlings' perfect messaging chain and they'd kick her out of the group for good.

The little voice of her conscience said, *Bring it on!*

Vanesa loved the challenge.

And besides, the twins' streak was more important.

"Let Emma and Eric get back, and I'll wait for the second round," Vanesa said.

"Are you sure?" Mami asked. "Your leg . . ."

"Mami," Vanesa said, waving her hand in the air. "I'll wait here, no problem."

"I'll wait with you," Beck said, stepping in her direction.

"It looks like it wasn't so bad in here after all if you guys don't want to leave," Beck's mom said.

Beck nodded. "I'm okay, Mom. I'll see you in a few."

Vanesa's mom held Hunter in her arms, enveloped in blankets. His long, skinny legs dangled from underneath them. One of his socks was coming off.

"Hurry!" Vanesa said. "The twins' birthday!"

Emma, Eric, and Mami—with Hunter in her arms—all rushed outside to the truck. Josiah was waiting with the engine on in case the truck decided it wouldn't wake up if it rested for even a few minutes. The snow was starting to fall again, and Bryce, who'd been leaning into the truck to talk with Josiah, looked up. He blinked and shook his head and said, "Son of a gun! A snowflake fell right in my eye!"

Vanesa and Beck exchanged a look, and they giggled as the truck drove back to the main lodge.

Bryce yawned and walked back into the lodge, followed by Rocky. Vanesa had realized that Rocky had a sense for telling who needed a little warmth and company the most. Now it was Bryce, because Beck and Vanesa had each other.

The newly minted friends snuggled on the sofa, and they covered themselves with a furry blanket that Vanesa hadn't noticed at the kids' lodge, but that she'd seen in one of Annabeth's portraits. The plaque at the lodge's entrance had told the truth—Annabeth really was the protector of Pinecloud, its inhabitants, *and* its guests.

Chapter Twenty-Six
When You Wish Upon a Deer

A little while later, Vanesa and Beck, wrapped in the shared blanket, ventured outside the lodge to wait for the truck. Vanesa pointed up at the sky, which had cleared in patches as the snow finally slowed down. A star seemed to peel from the dark velvet and fall behind the main lodge.

"Make a wish!" she said.

She didn't have time to choose one properly or even word it. The only thing she managed was picturing her brother safe and sound, watching his ninja cartoons or playing *DragonVille*.

Not a second later, Beck exclaimed, "Another one!"

Soon, the sky was streaked with shooting stars. Vanesa and Beck stopped pointing and oohing and ahing because the sky was so gorgeous, looking at it felt like being in a church or a museum or a sanctuary of greatness and beauty.

There was a rustling of leaves on the side of the cabin, and Vanesa turned to look. A shadow in the shape of a woman moved through the trees. Vanesa gasped when she saw the glow of silvery eyes. Beck turned to see what had scared Vanesa.

"Oh my gosh!" they said in amazed unison as a family of deer emerged from the darkness of the woods to cross the meadow.

The male was majestic. His antlers were covered in snow and tree leaves. He looked like the king of the forest. Closely behind him followed the female with their two babies. The little fawns crossed the meadow with shaky legs.

What Vanesa had thought was the shadow of a woman was actually the shadows and moonlight playing on the snow, but she loved the idea that one way or another, Annabeth was still in the forest, with the creatures she'd loved in life. The breeze blew a cloud away and ended the spell.

Vanesa's and Beck's eyes followed the family of deer until they got lost in the darkness of the woods behind the main lodge.

"Wow," Vanesa said. "It's like we're in a real-life fairy tale."

"That's why deer are my favorite animal," Beck said.

The girls stood silently, enchanted by the magic of what they had witnessed, until the truck came back for them. Bryce came outside then, yawning.

"So much energy, Bryce," Vanesa joked, and Bryce ruffled her hair.

"You kids are a high-maintenance group!" he said. "See you tomorrow for another ski lesson?"

"I think I need a break," Vanesa said, and Bryce winked at her.

Beck ran toward the truck, where Vanesa's dad was waiting with warm blankets and steaming cups. Papi got out and picked up Vanesa as if she didn't weigh more than a feather. But she was worried. "Where are Mami and Hunter?"

Papi placed her on the backseat, sat next to her, and hugged her against his side. He handed her the Styrofoam cup. Beautiful warmth and the scent of chocolate and cinnamon made Vanesa tear up.

"They went to the urgent care at the bottom of the hill," he said.

"Is Hunter okay?" Beck asked, her hands wrapped around her cup of cocoa.

Papi said, "Everything's under control, but of course Mami wanted to make sure."

Vanesa relaxed for the first time in hours. Her eyelids were so heavy. She closed her eyes for a second.

Papi said, "Let me hold this for you," and she didn't hear the rest because she felt like she was floating on a cloud, warm and content because she'd done the best that she could.

Chapter Twenty-Seven
Best Friends for Never

A bird was singing so happily, Vanesa heard it through the heavy barrier of a triple-pane glass window and layers and layers of exhaustion. But the cheerful trills brought her back from dreams of a magical deer and a house in the forest. Of friends looking at fireworks in the sky and brothers breathing the blue of the mountain air deeply.

Her eyes were still heavy when she opened them, but she felt alert.

She sat up. At first, she thought she was back in her room in California. But the sunshine was too bright. With the recent fires and the pollution, the sun in LA hadn't shone this bright in months. Besides, she didn't have a fancy fireplace back home. The events of the previous day came back to her in a rush.

Her luggage and Hunter's sat next to the door. With a sinking heart, she wondered if her parents had decided to cut their vacation short and go home after all that had happened. Maybe Hunter was very sick and they had no other choice.

She got up gingerly and put some weight on her foot. Her ankle felt much better. At least she could stand on it.

She changed out of her pajamas somberly, wanting to know about her brother, but dreading the moment that she'd talk to her parents.

Last night everyone had been happy that the kids had been safe and sound, but what would happen today when her mom and dad learned the truth? She'd broken more than one rule in going out into the storm. In the light of the day, her actions seemed rash and stupid.

Besides, what did Emma, Eric, and Beck think of her? She'd shown her real personality, without any filters or masks, and she was scared they wouldn't like the real Vanesa anymore.

When she put on her shoes—pink sneakers she didn't dare wear to school—she saw her phone resting on the coffee table in front of the fireplace with a note.

It's fully charged.

We went to lunch and will be in the rec room when you're ready to join us.

Love, Mami

Vanesa took a deep breath. Hunter must be okay if they were in the rec room. But then, why was their stuff all packed like they were ready to leave any minute? And now that she had her phone, she had no excuse to avoid looking at her messages from the Sunshine Darlings. She pressed the home button and got ready for a different kind of storm. She would gladly face another thundersnow storm than Amber's anger.

There were fifty-seven messages.

Fifty-six from Amber, and one from Peyton.

Vanesa thought about pretending the messages didn't exist. About ignoring Amber for the rest of her vacation and dealing with her when she went back to school. Or better yet, asking her parents to either switch her to a different school or homeschool her.

But no. Vanesa had crawled into a tiny door in a dark attic. She'd faced a snowstorm to find her brother and then to call for help. She could do this.

Still, opening the first message felt like sliding down a triple-black-diamond slope.

You have two minutes to reply to the thread or there will be consequences. Remember: Be a Darling.

Consequences? What did Amber know about consequences? What could she do to Vanesa after all? She was just a girl who thought she could control the world. Vanesa was done with being told that everything about her was wrong. As if belonging to the Darlings had made her life any better! Last night, without the constant pressure of her phone and the messages and the streaks, she felt free for the first time.

She didn't want to end up like . . . like Beck, with her fake friend, Vanessa.

She didn't need to fall into a pool to wake up from the nightmare of fake friends.

Vanesa laughed softly. Why hadn't she seen herself in the story Beck told her? Amber hadn't made a mean meme of her only because she never had the chance, but Vanesa knew she'd do it in a heartbeat.

Whatever consequences Amber had been thinking of, they had no hold on Vanesa anymore. Not after all that she'd been through the day before.

The other messages were more of the same; the language more ridiculous and abusive as the hours passed and Vanesa hadn't replied.

If you break our streak, I'll never forgive you and we'll kick you out of the club. How could you do this to us?

Vanesa sighed and reached the last words from Amber. The text had been sent at 10:01—that would have been 12:01 in Miami, where Amber was.

Why had Amber wasted her own vacation worrying about Vanesa so much? It sounded like the Darlings hadn't had a darling time in sunny Florida after all.

You're dead to us.

Below it was a picture of Amber and Rory throwing a golden friendship bracelet in the trash.

The words hurt, but when Vanesa looked at the picture, she realized Rory didn't have a convincing face. She looked like she was grimacing. And most telling of all was that Amber's eyes were red from crying. And no Peyton in the picture at all.

In spite of everything Amber had done and said to Vanesa, Vanesa felt bad for her. By the looks of it, she had alienated her friends the whole time, worried about what Vanesa was doing, trying to control her friends' lives since she had no say in her own.

Vanesa almost deleted Peyton's message without reading it. She was ready to put this behind her. She didn't need more hatred in her life. The Darlings had been clear. She was out of the group, and by the looks of it, the rest of the school year would be paying time for not accepting what Amber told her.

But she had a gut feeling, and if she'd learned one thing the previous day and night, it had been to listen to her instinct. So she opened the message.

It was brief, but it brought a ray of sunshine to Vanesa. She didn't need the validation anymore, but it was nice to know that Peyton was waking up from the enchantment of Amber and her empty threats and wanted to make her own decisions.

Vane, for what it's worth, you're not dead to me. I've always liked you, and I'd like to be your friend once we're back from spring break. I hope you're having fun on the slopes. No need to be chained to a streak, but if you can, send me pictures.

The old Vanesa whispered that this might be a trap.

Vanesa closed her eyes and tried to listen to the real Vanesa, the one who trusted and wanted to be trusted in exchange. And what she felt was that it was okay to give Peyton another chance.

She stood up, walked toward the window, and smiled as she watched a group of kids building a snowman, Rocky running in circles around them and wagging that tail like the happy dog he was.

She snapped a picture of him, captioned it *True happiness and love*, and sent it to Peyton. She also wrote *See you at school in a few days. I have to go. My friends and my brother are waiting for me.*

She clicked send, returned her phone to the spot on the table, and smiled.

Chapter Twenty-Eight
Par-Tay!

Vanesa grabbed the stuffed baby deer and ran down the stairs. Her ankle still hurt, so she slowed down. She was giddy thinking of seeing her new friends and going out into the snow with them for the greatest winter vacation of her life.

She didn't see Zachariah Grant standing at the bottom landing, and she crashed straight into him.

"Sorry!" they both said at the same time.

Vanesa laughed. "I'm sorry! I didn't see you!"

Zachariah winked at her. "That's something I haven't heard before."

From the main desk, Luís greeted her. "Boa tarde, Vanesa. Did you sleep well?" Gone was the stress from yesterday.

She glanced at the giant clock in the lobby, and she blushed. It wasn't the morning anymore. It was fifteen minutes past noon. She could say she'd slept quite all right.

"It was perfect," she said. She'd been so tired, she didn't care about sleeping on the trundle bed.

"I'm happy to hear," he said. "Now, I believe there's a party waiting for you in the recreation room at the end of the hallway."

"What kind of party?"

She felt bubbles in her head. She was so excited.

Zachariah said, "It's a surprise. Now hurry back!"

She didn't wait to be told twice. She hurried to the end of the hallway where she could hear Mami's favorite song playing and the sound of excited voices.

She opened the French doors and gasped at the wonderful sight. There were balloons and garlands everywhere. It was a mishmash of holidays: Halloween skulls next to toy Santa Clauses and elves mixed in with paper turkeys and even a Día de Muertos candy skull or two. Fourth of July banners and Valentine's hearts and baby cupids. Emma and Eric had paper crowns, and from the ceiling hung a make-shift piñata. It was a regular supermarket paper bag on which someone had painted a caricature of the five kids, Rocky the dog, Bryce, and even Annabeth.

Vanesa hobbled to Emma with open arms and cried, "Happy birthday! Oh my gosh, this is so perfect!"

Emma was beaming. She'd switched the beads on her braids to black and white.

Eric was beaming, too, wearing a basketball shirt with the face of his favorite *DragonVille* dragon, the green one, which was also Hunter's favorite.

"Did you see the shooting stars last night?" Vanesa asked.

"They were celebratory fireworks," said the twins' mom, Jennifer. She, too, had black-and-white beads in her hair.

Hunter came running toward Vanesa and wrapped his little arms around her waist. "You're alive! I thought you were like Sleeping Beauty, but Beck said you were just plain tired."

Beck was putting the finishing touches on the cake, a rectangular vanilla and chocolate with *Happy Birthday, Emma and Eric* written in loopy letters.

"Beck!" Vanesa called.

Beck's nose was bright pink, looking totally flechada by the sun. She smiled at Vanesa and said, "You're awake! I told Hunter you were just tired, but I was kind of worried, too."

Vanesa didn't know what to say. She stretched out her hand and offered the stuffed deer to Beck.

Beck's eyes lit up. She grabbed the deer and hugged it close. "Thank you," she said. She pulled out something from her pocket. It was a stuffed dog, the exact replica of Rocky. She offered it to Vanesa, and Vanesa hugged it close.

"A little reminder that your true friends see the inside, the real you," Beck said. Then she continued with the cake decorations.

"Thank you," Vanesa said. She was grateful not only for the dog but also for the trust Beck had shown in telling her the story about the other Vanessa.

Everything was as it should be.

Mami and Papi came up to Vanesa to ask if she'd slept well, if her leg hurt, how she felt. She hugged them both. "I'm sorry I ruined this vacation."

Papi pulled her back to look in her eyes and asked, "What do you mean?"

"Are we leaving?" she asked. "I don't want to go yet."

"Why do you think that?" Papi asked.

"Well, the suitcases . . ."

Mami laughed. "Although the first day was very eventful, to say the least, things wouldn't have turned out well if you hadn't followed your instincts, Vane." She kissed the top of Vanesa's head, and added, "I'm proud of you."

At that, Josiah Grant walked up to Vanesa and said, "The grand suite is open. Since the sofa isn't a worthy bed for our heroine, we thought you'd like to switch."

That's all she'd wanted yesterday when she arrived in the shuttle. To be alone in the room with her hot cocoa.

Now she looked around at her new friends, her heart bursting with love for all of them. She didn't want to be alone.

"What if Hunter and Beck moved in with me for the week? Would that be okay?" she asked.

Beck's face lit up, and she nodded. Her mom smiled behind her.

"We can arrange that!" said Josiah, and left—Vanesa assumed to inform Luís of the new arrangements.

"We're all here and we can celebrate!" said Eric.

Vanesa looked around, though, and realized two important people were missing.

In that moment, the back door opened with a bang, startling everyone, and after the dust of the snow had settled, a bear-like dog emerged. When *he* caught Vanesa's eye, he barked once in salute. Bryce followed him. He had dark bags under his eyes. He looked exhausted, but he still smiled.

Vanesa opened her arms for Rocky.

Still, he didn't run. He took the smallest, daintiest steps toward her. And when he reached her, she leaned down and kissed the top of his head.

"Now we're all here," she said, and they all gathered for a picture that would decorate the lodge for years to come.

Acknowledgments

Thank you, super-agent Linda Camacho, for your faith in my stories and in my ability to bring them to life. #TeamCamacho forever.

Thanks to Olivia Valcarce and Aimee Friedman for helping me carve an idea into a story I'm proud to share with the world, and to the whole team at Scholastic, especially Jana Haussman, Jael Fogle, Nora Milman, Jennifer Rinaldi, and Wendy Dopkin.

Suma Subramanian and Aída Salazar, your friendship, insight, guidance, and support mean so much to me! Thank you!

Courtney Alameda, thanks for reminding me to *above all else, remain true to myself.*

To mis amigas del alma: July, Veeda, Karina, Iris, y Anedia. Chicas, las quiero! Gracias totales.

Kassidy and Verónica, thank you for all your help and love. I could never write my stories without you.

Ruby Cochran-Simms, my English teacher, who would have thought? I'm forever grateful.

Otto, gracias for answering all my questions about California and for being a great friend.

To my family (Jeff, Juli, Maga, Joax, Lel, Valen, Nova, Dandi, y Coco) gracias for your aguante and love, and for being an endless source of inspiration. Also to my siblings, Damián, Belén, y Lalo. Lo hice!

A todos los chicos y familias del 7 de Septiembre, los llevo en mi corazón para siempre.

My writing communities at the Vermont College of Fine Arts, VONA, We Need Diverse Books, WIFYR, Storymakers, and the Kidlit Authors of Color group, this book wouldn't exist without you!

And last, but not least, my gratitude and love to the infinite beauty of the mountains, valleys, deserts, and forests in Utah. Your winters are so long, but you're so rad!

Find more reads you will love . . .

Dacey Culpepper Biel comes from a long line of pie bakers. But Dacey didn't inherit a gift for baking. Even worse? Business at her family's pie shop has been slow, and the only person who might be able to help is Dacey's arch-rival, the cute Chayton Freedel. When clues arise about a long-hidden pie recipe, Dacey will have to work alongside Chayton. Can she find the recipe *and* save her family's legacy?